WHAT HAPPENED TO RACHEL RILEY?

CLAIRE SWINARSKI

Quill Tree Books
An Imprint of HarperCollinsPublishers

Quill Tree Books is an imprint of HarperCollins Publishers.

What Happened to Rachel Riley?
Copyright © 2023 by Claire Swinarski
All rights reserved. Printed in the United States of America.

www.harpercollinschildrens.com

Library of Congress Cataloging-in-Publication Data

Names: Swinarski, Claire, author.
Title: What happened to Rachel Riley? / Claire Swinarski.
Description: First edition. | New York, NY : Quill Tree Books, [2023]
  | Audience: Ages 8-12. | Audience: Grades 4-6. | Summary:
  "Thirteen-year-old new girl Anna Hunt decides to make an
  investigative podcast about how fellow classmate Rachel Riley went
  from being the most popular girl in school to the most hated"—
  Provided by publisher.
Identifiers: LCCN 2022021827 | ISBN 978-0-06-321309-8 (hardcover)
Subjects: CYAC: Sexual harassment—Fiction. | Bullies and bullying—
  Fiction. | Podcasts—Fiction. | Middle schools—Fiction. | Schools—
  Fiction.
Classification: LCC PZ7.1.S9477 Wh 2023 | DDC [Fic]—dc23
LC record available at https://lccn.loc.gov/2022021827

22 23 24 25 26 LBC 5 4 3 2 1

First Edition

TO EIGHTH-GRADE GIRLS
EVERYWHERE

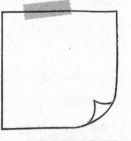

DECEMBER 23

Ms. O'Dell,

I hope that you're having a good winter break. Enclosed you will find my un-essay for our Social Issues class. I'm sorry it's late, but I hope you understand. Thanks for giving me an Incomplete on my report card instead of an F, because that would have given my mom a heart attack.

When you first asked us to do an un-essay, I didn't know what to think. I thought maybe it was because I was new and we didn't have things like un-essays in Chicago. We only had . . . actual essays. But then I realized it wasn't because I was new, it was because nobody in all of East Middle's current eighth grade had done an un-essay before.

I really liked Social Issues, even though some people in this un-essay would disagree and call it

1

a "waste of taxpayer dollars." No offense—their words, not mine. I liked that you let us choose our own topic, too.

I know other kids worked on topics that seem bigger or more important, like capital punishment or immigration. But you said it just had to be any social question that mattered to us, and that it didn't have to be trending on Twitter or covered on the news.

So I asked what happened to Rachel Riley.

Enclosed you will find the results of my research. In addition to my notebook, you will also find one pair of swim trunks, an old iPhone with recorded interviews, a gift certificate for Lee's Dairy Emporium, a purple lighter, a stapled packet of text message transcripts, and a pack of hallway passes. The passes were stolen from Mr. Corey's desk in the art room—you can return them if you want.

I hope you learn, from everything in this box, how Rachel Riley went from being the most popular girl in school to a Complete Social Outcast of the First Degree. I also hope you learn that when asking a complicated question, you should prepare for that question to shake and quake into a thousand more. Because people, like fires, can surprise you. And lies, like flames, can spread faster than we can put them out.

Sincerely,
Anna Hunt
Eighth Grade Social Issues
East Middle School

≍1≍

THE UN-ESSAY

MS. O'DELL
ROOM 912

Assignment: This semester in Social Issues, you will be required to complete a semester-long project instead of a final exam. This project will take the form of an "un-essay." That means you can do anything on a social topic of your choosing, as long as it *isn't* an essay.

Past examples from former students:
- Visiting a prison and interviewing an incarcerated person
- Shadowing a law enforcement officer for a day and creating a documentary about your experience
- Creating a podcast about your family's immigration experience

- Designing a pamphlet about the lack of feminine hygiene products for girls around the globe
- Launching a community garden to make a statement about climate change and urban development

Get creative: You can use sewing, cooking, painting, or any other medium that will help you explore a social issue and translate it for our class.

Remember: Social issues don't have to be things that are widely covered in the news. In fact, some of the most interesting stories are the ones that aren't being told. They can be small or large, local or international. Think of something that's interesting to *you*—you'll be working on this project for the entirety of our first semester, so try and make it something you're passionate about!

Grade: Your un-essay will be worth 85 percent of your final grade. Assignments will be graded on thoroughness, creativity, and presentation.

SEPTEMBER 8

HI, MS. O'DELL . . . THIS IS ANNA HUNT. OBVIOUSLY. You said you wanted us to share a little bit more about ourselves to get to know us, so . . . here's that recording you asked for. It's cool that you didn't just want us to, like, write a note or whatever. I kind of feel like I'm making a podcast or something.

Anyway, there's not that much to tell. I'm new to East this year. I'm twelve years old. I know that's young for eighth grade, but I started kindergarten early because I was kind of smart for a kid. I mean, I'm still a kid, but whatever. When I was *little*. I used to live in Chicago, but we moved up here to Madison because my mom's going to teach at the University of Wisconsin Law School this semester. My dad is a lawyer, too, but he just works from our living room and writes contracts for companies. Oh, and I have a sister named Nik, who is a sophomore at East High. She's, like, a total tech genius. She already designed her own app that can play different sounds, like crickets or waves, when you sleep. Her real name is Nikola, which is kind of a unique name around here, but my mom is from Poland. We speak Polish, too, which is fun, because there were lots of Polish people in Chicago but there aren't many here, so it's like we have a secret language. I don't have a big extended family or anything, but my grandma does still live in Poland, and I talk to her a lot.

Anyway . . . I'm really not that interesting. I like to read, and I have two dogs named Jesse and Kix. I like cooking with my dad. I don't play sports or anything like that, so . . . I guess that's kind of all you need to know.

I've been trying to think about my Social Issues project, but I know we have a little more time to decide. I'll try to pick a topic soon.

SEPTEMBER 9

To: LIST: Parents of East Eighth Graders

From: Principal Lila Howe <lhowe@east.middle.edu>

Subj: Today's lunchroom incident

Parents of East Middle School Eighth Graders,

It is with great disappointment that I must write to you and address the unfortunate incident that took place during today's eighth-grade lunch period.

First, let me remind you that East Middle School has a culture of peace. But our school motto, "Peace begins with us," was under attack during today's altercation in the cafeteria.

It's been widely reported that the first projectile in the food fight was a carton of milk, which some parents have pointed out may have been in protest of, or social commentary on, the use of dairy factory farm products in our school. Not so, I assure you! The original item that was thrown was not a dairy product at all. The students appreciate the fact that Kincaid Farms has been supplying our school with milk for decades! Even after the terrible situation that unfolded surrounding last year's awards ceremony, our relationship with Kincaid Farms remains loud and proud.

The student who instigated today's events has been spoken to, and his parents have been notified. Please continue discussing the idea of peace with your East Knight at home.

We at East Middle School know we will rise stronger than ever—together!

Best,
Lila Howe

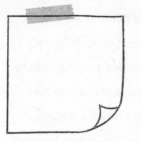

SEPTEMBER 9

Dear Principal Howe,

    This is my note of apology for starting the food fight. I'm sorry. I apologized to Riz already, but just so you know, it was only because he made a joke about me having a crush on Rachel Riley, which I don't, and that was a really bogus thing to say. I would never have a crush on her. But he doesn't have to write a letter of apology, which is unfair. It's important for you to have all of the facts.

    Sincerely,

    Blake Wyatt

    Eighth Grade

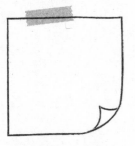

SEPTEMBER 10

Dear Principal Howe,

    I got your email that said an apology followed by "but" isn't an apology. Here is my new apology note.

    I am sorry that I threw a hamburger at Riz Kapoor.

    Sincerely,

    Blake Wyatt

    Eighth Grade

VOICE RECORDING

SEPTEMBER 13

HI, MS. O'DELL. SO I KNOW OUR VOICE RECORDINGS of our assignments are due today . . . and I had a really hard time picking what to do. I'm interested in a lot of stuff about the world, but it all just felt so big. People have been trying to solve world hunger and climate change for years and years. Like, our own government can't even figure out how to solve these issues. How was I going to do a project on one of them?

But then I remembered you said it could be something small, something more . . . local.

And it got me thinking.

At lunch, Principal Howe reads off all of the names of people whose birthday it is. You probably know this because sometimes you're a lunch supervisor. Anyway, when she reads a name, people cheer. Obviously, the popular kids get the loudest cheers. When Jordan

Russell's name was read last week, I thought the building was going to fall over. She seems pretty popular, and *everyone* likes her since she's nice, too. But no matter what, every name that's called gets at least *some* cheers, because everyone has *some* friends— even the nerds cheer for each other. No offense. I'm kind of a nerd myself, if you want me to be honest.

So, what's funny is that today's my birthday. Birthdays when you're a new kid kind of suck. Nobody decorated my locker or anything, because I don't have any friends yet. And eighth grade is a little old to bring birthday treats or whatever. So I'm just, like, sitting in math class like any other day, even though it's my thirteenth birthday. And then at lunch, I was sitting by myself, which is just so awkward, and I know I could ask to sit with some other kids, but whatever. I just feel weird. They all have their seats, and what if they said no? Then, what, I'm just standing there?

Sorry. This is a long recording.

Anyway, it's my birthday, and Principal Howe read my name over the loudspeaker. And people actually clapped, because some people clap for everyone. Bee Becker, who sits next to me in French, turned around and looked at me all surprised, and I think she felt kind of bad because she didn't say anything in class earlier. But I wasn't mad, because, duh, how would anyone know? She let out a little cheer. So I had some noise, and people barely know me.

Then Principal Howe read the next name: Rachel Riley.

And nobody did *anything*. Not a single person clapped for her! It was so, so weird—like, total silence. Nobody was even *talking* . . . I mean, it was so strange. She didn't have a single person who would even pity clap for her? Even though there were people who would cheer for *me*? I should have started, probably—but I was so surprised, all I could do was sit there. It was almost eerie. And before I knew it, the next name was being called.

Rachel Riley is in my algebra class. I know who she is. I looked over to where she was sitting, and she was just, like, eating her apple like nothing had happened. Like nobody had said her name. And I felt really bad for her. Nobody should have to eat an apple alone on their birthday and be embarrassed like that.

Principal Howe moved on, but I just—I don't know. It got me thinking. If people would cheer for a person they don't even know, but wouldn't for Rachel Riley, it wasn't that she didn't have friends. It was that she had enemies.

Everyone.

Then something even weirder happened.

I was walking to the bathroom after lunch, and I passed the trophy case. I don't know why I've never stopped to look at it before, but today I did. And sitting inside was a photo of the dance team. You know who was front and center?

Rachel Riley.

I guess they won junior state last year. And everyone's arms were thrown around her, and they were all laughing. They looked so happy. She didn't *look* like a girl who wouldn't get any cheers on her birthday.

So *then*, I looked her up on Instagram. And you know what I saw?

Photos. Tons of them. Her and Jordan Russell, her and Kaylee Nakamura, her and *everyone*. It looked like she had a ton of friends! Until May 20, last spring. At the end of seventh grade. That's the last photo. And it's just a selfie of her, smiling at the camera.

So here's the question I'd like to explore:

What happened to Rachel Riley?

SEPTEMBER 13

To: Alicia O'Dell <aodell@east.middle.edu>

From: Maja Hunt <mhunt@wisc.edu>

Subj: RE: Anna's Social Issues assignment

Alicia,

Thanks for reaching out about Anna's proposed project. I understand your concerns—that you don't wish for the student in question to feel ostracized—and I appreciate your active involvement in my daughter's education. But after looking closely at the assignment sheet she was provided, I see the exact phrase: *a social topic of your choosing.*

Thus, your appeal for her to "consider another topic" seem to be contrary to the original assignment, unless you are willing to concede that your original assignment contained a false suggestion.

While Anna recognizes, as do I, the importance of sensitivity surrounding this matter, she believes it could speak to a larger trend of bullying, ostracization, and inclusion among the student body. We are willing to pursue Anna's right to an un-essay of her choosing through whatever legal avenues necessary. Or you could simply allow her to comply with the original assignment as intended.

Peace begins with us, after all.

Sincerely,
Maja Hunt, Attorney-at-Law
Professor
University of Wisconsin–Madison

SEPTEMBER 14

To: Maja Hunt <mhunt@wisc.edu>

From: Alicia O'Dell <aodell@east.middle.edu>

Subj: RE: Anna's Social Issues assignment

Maja,

While I appreciate your passion for your daughter's education, I simply can't allow a project to be done on another student's popularity. Anna seems incredibly bright—I'm sure she'll think of another topic she's just as interested in.

I've cc'd our principal, Lila Howe. You can direct all future legal inquiries to her.

Sincerely,

Alicia O'Dell

East Middle School

"I CAN'T FIGURE THIS THING OUT," I MUTTERED, TRY-ing to plug the cord from my phone to my computer. For some reason, my favorite podcast wasn't showing its latest episode, so I was trying to download it from my laptop. I just kept getting an error message.

Every Tuesday, I went on a long walk just to listen to the latest episode of *Stories of Our Lives with Mimi Miller*. Mimi interviewed all kinds of people, and not just famous people, even though the episode where she interviewed Kate Middleton about her charity work was my favorite. Mimi also talked to totally everyday men and women. She spoke with janitors and chefs and teachers and stay-at-home parents about who they were and what mattered to them. People who lived in mansions and people experiencing homelessness. People you walked by every day or sat a table over from at Red Robin. The way Mimi really got to the heart of who a person was, and what they were all about? It made everyone seem . . . real. It made you think about people differently. Like that girl who's being mean at school, or that guy who's yelling at the grocery store worker, or the woman who lives under the bridge down by campus with her four dogs. You started to understand that they had a whole story behind them, bigger than this one moment you were looking at.

Maybe Rachel Riley was bigger than East Middle School. In fact, I was sure of it. That was why I had wanted to do a podcast about her for my un-essay. Just like Mimi Miller would.

"Do you need help?" My older sister, Nik, glanced up from her laptop and pulled down her headphones. Nikola Hunt: sixteen, genius, can't name any bands from the last ten years but can rattle off her five favorite pieces of software to use for coding. Me: still googles "East Middle School email login" because I can never remember the URL.

"No," I said. Whenever Nik helped me with a tech thing, I ended up feeling like an idiot.

"Did you try unplugging it and replugging it in?"

"I said I don't need help," I grumbled as I did what she told me to do. With a *ba-doop*, Apple Podcasts popped up on my computer. She grinned smugly, and I stuck my tongue out at her.

"How old are you, five?" she responded. "What are you doing, anyway?"

"Trying to get Mimi Miller to download. Aren't

you supposed to be, like, a younger Mark Zuckerberg? Telling someone to unplug and replug—*I* could have thought of that."

"Yeah, but you *didn't*. And almost anything works better when you unplug it for a second."

"Girls," Mom yelled from the kitchen, "butts in chairs, please. Dinner." Maja Hunt: intense lawyer lady, crushes bad guys in her sleep, secretly loves any and all Pixar movies. I bounded out of the living room and was hit with the smell of spaghetti sauce. Dad was whistling to himself, ladling sauce on huge plates of pasta. Jamie Hunt: part-time lawyer, full-time Dad/chef/laundry folder. My parents were the kind of parents who thought if we didn't eat family dinners together we'd wind up criminal masterminds or something.

That was my family, or *rodzina*, as Babcia would say.

"Ooh, fancy. Sauce that's not from a jar," I said.

Dad flicked me in my temple. "You're welcome."

"Nik, can you feed the dogs quick?" Mom asked, grabbing a piece of garlic bread and doing the *ouch, ouch, too hot* dance before dropping it onto her plate. "And Anna . . . did you think of a new topic for Social Issues yet?"

"What project?" asked Nik.

21

"It's, like . . . It's called an un-essay. My teacher's kind of weird. But nice."

"She has the kids doing these voice recordings for assignments on their phones, and then they upload them to a class RSS feed. It's actually pretty cool," Mom told Nik.

"Anyway, I have to do a creative project on a social topic of my choosing—"

"Key phrase," Mom said smugly.

". . . and I wanted to do it on a girl at school."

"English!" Dad called from the counter. Oops. Mom, Nik, and I were speaking Polish to each other—it was kind of like our secret language, since Dad didn't know much more than the basics. He said you have to learn languages like that when you're a kid, or else your vocal cords fully develop and it's hard to be able to make the right sounds. Mom says he just doesn't want to have to practice every day. Half the time, we didn't even realize when we slipped into Polish around him.

"Sorry, Dad," Nik said—in English. "You're doing a project on a girl at school?"

"No. I mean—kind of. It's about . . . I don't know, bullying. Social classes."

"A middle school caste system," said Mom, pointing a fork at me.

"Yes. *Exactly*." I nodded, grabbing some bread for myself.

"The haves and the have-nots," Dad said, getting the Parmesan cheese from the fridge and bringing it to the table. The real stuff, not the kind in the plastic cylinder from the store. Yum.

"Rachel Riley is definitely a have-not," I said. "Everyone hates her. But they didn't used to. And I wanted to find out why."

"Ostracization by society. Important stuff," Dad said.

"It doesn't matter. Ms. O'Dell won't let me do it," I said.

"Sorry, bud. I tried. I can't flex my legal muscles too many times or *I'll* be the ostracized one at parent-teacher conferences," Mom said. "And do you really want to tick kids off, anyway? It's a new school. Maybe make a friend or two before you start harassing everyone."

Mom was always on my case about making *friends*, like I was some kind of social leper. I had friends back in Chicago. I had Kateri, from youth group, and Sabrina, my lab partner. I wasn't, like, class president or head cheerleader or anything. I just—didn't care about a lot of the stuff other kids cared about, like the latest TikTok trend or whose mom had bought her a

Kate Spade purse. I was known as That Weird Girl Who Reads a Lot, the way you can be known as That Girl Who's Super Tall or That Girl Who Wears a Ton of Lip Gloss or That Quiet Girl.

That's how I knew: people thought I was just a little . . . different. I didn't want to talk about which girl was invited to another girl's birthday party. I spent a lot of lunch hours in the library, reading, because who wouldn't rather be in the Kingdom of Norta from the Red Queen series than middle school? I liked *books*. Was that so different?

So, no, I wasn't Miss Popular with a long list of friends I could call at any moment. I wasn't a mega-genius, like Nik, or super outgoing, like Mom, or a great listener, like Dad.

But I had people to clap for me on my birthday, unlike Rachel Riley.

"Why do you even care?" Nik asked, sprinkling extra salt on her spaghetti.

"Because I'm a human being, not a computer chip," I snapped at her.

Nik could be obnoxious. It was pretty much a Big Sister Requirement. But she sort of had a point, I thought, as I twirled my spaghetti around my fork. Why *did* I even care about Rachel Riley?

I don't know.

But here's what I did know: My very first day of school? It was hard. Being the new kid felt like walking around all day with pants that were four sizes too tight. I couldn't breathe easily or stop feeling uncomfortable, and I just couldn't wait to get home. I couldn't even find my homeroom, and none of the wings of the school made sense. Where was upper A wing, and why wasn't it above lower A wing? That would make *sense*, right? And I started blinking—fast, really fast. That almost-gonna-cry fast, but being the new kid had enough problems. I didn't need to start crying in the middle of the hallway.

"Upper A wing is above the commons," a voice said. I looked over at the girl who was speaking. Looked *down*, really, because she was pretty short. Blonde hair that just touched her shoulders, and a really cool jacket. Like a detective's trench coat, but purple. Sparkly shoes. Kind eyes.

"What?"

She nodded toward a staircase. "You look confused. I just figured—upper B is on top of lower A, and it makes no sense. Are you looking for your homeroom?"

"Um . . . yeah."

She glanced at my schedule. "A3. Upper A. Those

25

stairs, on the left. Mrs. Orcason has her door deco-rated like an ocean floor . . . *Orca*son, get it?"

I just nodded.

And then she was gone, the scent of apple sham-poo lingering behind her.

Not every eighth-grade girl stops and helps a new kid about to burst into tears find their homeroom.

And if they do, they deserve some applause on their freaking birthday.

After I helped Dad pack up the leftover pasta sauce and wash the dishes, I did a deep-dive audit of other kids' Instagrams and TikToks. It wasn't hard—I just looked at who Rachel was following. *She* had only eleven followers—and about half of them looked to be bots. The other half had the last name Riley, so I guessed they were cousins or something.

But she still followed a ton of kids from school. Jordan Russell, Kaylee Nakamura, Riz Kapoor. I couldn't believe how many of them had public profiles. Mom and Dad made me keep everything private. If I scrolled back far enough, I saw her—Rachel. Smiling, laughing, dancing in TikTok videos she had uploaded to Reels. Buried in sand next to Kaylee and Jordan on the beach, with just their blonde, brown, and black buns poking out.

Well. At least I knew where to start: with Kaylee and Jordan. I reached over to shut off my lamp and drifted off to sleep.

2

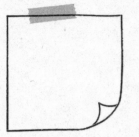

SEPTEMBER 15

Jordan—

What's up? If Mr. Krall-Ryan gives us more homework tonight I'm gonna totally freak out! Nutcracker tryouts are in two weeks, and I need extra rehearsal time every night for ballet. I don't have time for pre-algebra, lol. OMG that new girl Hannah is kind of weird. Outside after lunch she just came up to me and started talking to me like we were best friends. And then she was asking me about Rachel and I was like, um, I am NOT friends with her lol. Like why does she even care about some random loser?! Get a life.

Xoxo

Kaylee

Kaylee—

Lol I know. His favorite hobby is grading our homework. Like, play a sport or something!!! Or get a GF. Maybe we should make him a dating app profile haha. Does he seem more the Bumble or Farmers Only type?

You think she's weird?? I kind of like her. I'm pretty sure it's Anna, not Hannah. I have English with her, and we sit next to each other. I wonder why she wants to know about Rachel. You didn't say anything to her, did you?

OxOx

Jordan

Jordan—

Duh! No!!!!!

I mean she was nice or whatever. Just kind of nosy. Like, she started by inviting me to her house this weekend, and I was like, oh cool! Yeah! She probably needs friends and I was trying to be nice. But then she's all like, yeah, I thought maybe you me and Rachel? Like she was trying to see how I reacted. So I said, um, no, I don't hang out with her. But that's all I would say.

I should have told her to ask you . . . you are the one who has the MOST right to be mad!

Xoxo

Kaylee

Kaylee—

Do NOT bring me up to her! Please! I just don't ever want to think about Rachel Riley again.

OxOx

Jordan

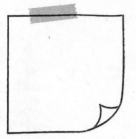

Mr. Krall-Ryan,

I am sorry that I was writing notes in class. I will not do it again. Thank you for not reading the note in front of the class.

Sincerely,

Jordan Russell

Northwestern University Campus for Kids Announces

SUMMER REPORTING CAMP

Are you . . .

- Between the ages of thirteen and sixteen?

- The kind of kid who spends all day listening to *Serial*, *This American Life*, and *Story of Our Lives*?

- Interested in exploring the world of digital media production?

If so, you're invited to apply to the Northwestern's Campus for Kids Podcasting Summit!

For two weeks, you can spend your mornings on the beautiful NU campus, craft a podcast on a topic of your choice, and be mentored by award-winning journalist Mimi Miller. Campers will leave the summit with a fully produced miniseries, a working knowledge of the ever-changing digital media frontier, and the experience of a lifetime. Each miniseries will then be released on Blink, an exciting new podcasting network exclusively for teens created by Miller.

The summit will only accept ten participants to allow each podcaster enough assistance and access.

To apply, teens must fill out the application and have it signed by a parent or legal guardian. Applications must also include a forty-minute-long podcasting sample. This does not need to be professionally produced—that's what the summit is for! But it should demonstrate a passion for people, a willingness to ask tough questions, and a gift for storytelling.

Applications are due December 31. Good luck!

SEPTEMBER 15

To: Katarzyna Kowalski <babciakat@gmail.com>

From: Anna Hunt <ahunt@east.middle.edu>

Subj: New email

Babcia,

Here's my new email address! New everything: school, house, city, email . . . it's a lot.

I'm glad we got to FaceTime last night. I know you don't know how to work your new phone so well, but it was really nice to actually see your face! And thanks for your support about my Rachel Riley project. But Ms. O'Dell won't budge.

You know what, though? I still wanted to find out what happened to her. This is probably where Mom would tell me to drop it—and she kind of did, actually. So I told Ms. O'Dell I was going to do a project on recycling. I'll do a collage or something. But I'm still going to investigate. Like on *Serial*. I can't just *let* this girl walk around with everyone hating her. What if we all just *let* the bad things around us keep going and going and going? Besides, it'll be good practice if I want to be the next Sarah Koenig. I'm even going to use this podcast to apply to a summer program in Chicago where I'd get to make a *real* show with Mimi Miller—you know she's my hero. But please-please-please don't tell my parents . . . I'll cross that bridge when I get accepted. *If* I get accepted—I bet tons of kids are applying. Plus, the age limit goes all the way up to sixteen. How am I supposed to compete with people who can drive around to get interviews?

So, I talked to Rachel Riley. I sat down next to her at lunch yesterday. And let's just say you'll have an easier time talking to Nik when she's knee-deep in her precious code than you will getting five words out of Rachel Riley. But I saw an opening. Rachel Riley usually pulls out a book and reads at lunch, and yesterday was no different. I mean, anyone who reads a book at lunch is my kind of friend, right? I glanced up at her, scooted down a few feet so I was right across from her, and took a deep breath.

"So . . . what are you reading?"

She looked up at me slowly, over the cover of her book. And just stared.

"I like to read, too," I said. You *know* that's true. You give me a book every year for Christmas. I loved the one you gave me last year, about the girl my age during World War II.

"*Wonder*," she said. "About this kid who was born with a facial difference. It's really good."

I told her I'd heard about it. I was pretty sure Kateri had checked it out from the library once. Then I reminded her who I was—that she had given me directions the first day of school.

"Oh yeah," she said. She was glad I found my homeroom. She asked me what other classes I had, and I told her. She wasn't in my Social Issues class—she's taking art metals instead—so I kind of explained the assignment, and then . . . I told her.

That I had originally wanted to do it on *her*.

And I felt bad for half a second, because her face kind of fell. Babcia, it was like I'd hurt her feelings or something. So

I started to talk super fast about how I felt like there was an injustice being done, like some kind of whole anti-Rachel *thing* going on, and that I had wanted to help her figure out why. But then—guess what she said!

"I know why."

She *knew* why?!

"Well . . . why?" I asked her. And by now, I was confused. Had she done something super horrible to everybody? If so, why didn't she just apologize?

She just looked at me for a second, and I could tell she was deciding something. She had that look people get on their faces when they're at the grocery store, deciding whether they're going to go for the real vanilla ice cream or those fat-free frozen bars Mom and Dad get sometimes. That look of *thought*, you know? Weighing calories vs. taste.

"I'm not going to tell you," she said. "You want to know, you can figure it out yourself."

I didn't even know what to say. And then the bell rang, so everyone had to either go outside for "outdoor time," which is basically recess but we all just stand around and talk, or you can go to the library and do your homework. So Rachel Riley left the cafeteria and took off down the hallway.

It's a mystery, is what I'm trying to say. Like that show you like about the teacher who becomes a private investigator? That's going to be me.

And I decided something, too. I decided that I like Rachel Riley. Any girl who's not afraid to read a book at lunch right there in the middle of the cafeteria is all right by me.

I miss you so, so, so, so much. I hope you can come for Christmas. Mom said you were thinking about it. I'll take you all over Madison. They even have rum raisin ice cream at Ella's Deli, and I know that's your favorite.

In science, we get to pick an animal that we'll do all these different projects on over the course of the year. I went with penguins. Remember when we visited them at the aquarium in Krakow, and Mom did all of those funny voices? Nik laughed so hard her soda came out of her nose.

Love,
Anna

SEPTEMBER 16

This is WHAT HAPPENED TO RACHEL RILEY?: THE MOST IMPORTANT MYSTERY TO HIT MIDDLE SCHOOL SINCE . . .

Wait, that sounds dumb. I'll just—

This is WHAT HAPPENED TO RACHEL RILEY?: AN INVESTIGATIVE PODCAST BY ANNA HUNT.

Whatever. Cut. I'll figure that part out later.

Here's the truth—I have no idea what happened to Rachel Riley because I can't get anywhere.

I started out by talking to Kaylee Nakamura, because I can tell from Instagram that she and Rachel used to be really good friends. But she totally clammed up when I even mentioned Rachel. Then, I thought I'd try to talk to Jordan Russell, who also seemed like she used to be her friend, but it felt almost like she knew what I was doing. Every time I've tried to talk to her, she kind of disappears. It's so weird. Like, we were outside after lunch and I tried to walk over to her, and suddenly she had to go to the bathroom. And then the next day, when I went up to her again, she ran inside. I overheard her telling the lunch aid that she needed her sweatshirt from her locker. But it was, like, eighty degrees. So I don't know what's up with that.

I think next I'm going to try Bee Becker. She sits next to me in French and seems pretty nice, so I'll bring it up during class, if I can do it without anybody else listening.

This has been Anna Hunt. Over and out.

SEPTEMBER 16

To: Sierra Kincaid <skincaid@kincaidfarms.com>
From: Principal Lila Howe <lhowe@east.middle.edu>
Subj: Cease and desist

Sierra,

I completely understand your reluctance to host our Harvest
Fest fundraiser this year after last year's unfortunate incident.
But I was shocked to hear you'd go so far as to refer to our
students as the Flamethrowers of East to our entire Zumba
class. I exercise to sweat off the stress of students, not be
reminded of them.

The student in question was adequately punished. The
seventh-grade class lost their Spring Fling. And insurance
more than covered the damages—or so I'm guessing, since

I saw your latest Instagram post about your venue being featured in *Midwest Weddings.*

Regards,
Lila Howe

BEE BECKER HAD BLONDE HAIR SO LONG SHE COULD sit on it if she wanted to. Instead, she wore it in a thick braid tossed over her shoulder, and sometimes she chewed on the end of it when she was nervous. I knew this because I saw her gnawing on it during our first French pop quiz. But right now, she didn't seem nervous at all. In fact, she seemed super calm, like she'd just gotten out of a meditation session or something.

"Why are you asking *me*?" Bee questioned, raising an eyebrow, and I felt stupid. I guess I was asking her about Rachel because I felt like maybe we were kind-of-sort-of becoming friends. When you're the new kid, the girl who sits next to you in French and is usually nice to you is the best you can get, sometimes.

"I just . . . I'm just wondering. Why everyone doesn't like her. She seemed nice to me, the first day of school."

Bee's eyes flickered down to my notebook. I moved

my hand as fast as I could, but it was too late—she'd seen the Northwestern application.

"I saw that, too," she said. "Mimi Miller shared it on TikTok."

"You follow Mimi Miller?" I asked, surprised.

"Yeah. She did an episode from the Hype House once. It was, like, really interesting. Anyway . . . are you applying?"

"Um. Maybe." I cleared my throat. The real answer? I couldn't *not* apply. If I wanted to tell stories like Mimi Miller did, I *had* to get into the summer program at Northwestern.

And the Rachel Riley project would make a perfect application.

"What's your podcast going to be on?" she asked.

"Well . . ." I said. "Rachel, kind of."

Oops. Oops, oops, oops. Abort mission. But it was too late—maybe a normal person wouldn't have noticed it: that flicker across Bee's bright blue eyes, that spark of realization. But I notice things other people don't. I always have. And I noticed that.

Bee Becker absolutely knew why nobody liked Rachel Riley.

"Wow. That's an intense idea," she said. We were supposed to be making progress on a worksheet with a long list of French verbs together, but I'd gotten it done in, like, fifteen seconds and then just let her copy me. "I mean, you can be friends with her if you want. Nobody's stopping you."

"I know . . . but—I guess I'm just wondering, was she mean to people? Is that why nobody likes her?"

"No. And I meant what I said—you can be friends with her. But . . . I wouldn't. That's all," Bee said calmly.

"What do you—"

"Brianna-Marie. Anna. *Faites attention, s'il vous plaît.*" Madam Hummel snapped her fingers. Around us, the rest of class was turning in their worksheets.

"I got it," I mumbled, grabbing our sheets. I was frustrated—I hadn't really gotten anywhere useful with Bee. My investigative reporting wasn't exactly Mimi Miller–worthy.

As I got to the front of the room and put our sheet on the pile, I glanced back at Bee. She was chewing on her braid as if she hadn't eaten in days, and she was texting, too.

Something had shaken her up. Something, I'd bet, that had to do with Rachel Riley.

I don't know why I'd thought I could trust Bee Becker. But by lunch, it was obvious: every single person knew about my podcast project. I could feel their

44

eyes on me, tracking me as I sat at my usual table and opened up the Ziploc bag I'd shoved a peanut butter sandwich into that morning. I felt them staring as I quickly ate and tossed my trash, too. *Everyone's* eyes, even the lunch lady's. And I swear, I could hear whispers. My skin tingled hot; if someone touched me, I felt like I'd shock them.

And then she said . . .

. . . why does she . . .

. . . asking questions . . .

. . . new kid . . .

. . . Rachel Riley . . .

And there she sat. On the other end of my table, on the opposite side, slowly eating her own peanut butter sandwich and reading a book. I glanced at her, and she met my eyes for a second.

Then she went back to her book.

The entire popular table seemed to be laughing just a little louder and whispering just a little more than usual. You can just *tell*, sometimes, who the kids are that everyone else is watching. Jordan Russell and Kaylee Nakamura, plus a handful of obnoxious boys who always played basketball during outdoor time. It wasn't just their table, though. It was also the table of kids who spent lunch drawing anime, and the table of kids who always wore athletic shorts and had soccer pins on their backpacks, and the table of kids whose faces were on the posters for student government campaigns. It felt like all of those tables were peering at me, wondering what I was *doing*, investigating Rachel Riley.

There went my chance at being normal. At making friends. At not being the weird girl who was a year younger and read books at lunch, sharing a table with Rachel Riley. Why couldn't I have just let it go? If I wanted to do a podcast so badly, I could just do one on recycling and make *that* my project. Ms. O'Dell loved recycling. Five other kids were doing projects on it.

Here's why, though: because it's easier to throw a water bottle in the right bin than it is to not be a jerk in middle school. Who was I supposed to interview? The mayor? Rinse out your spaghetti sauce jars before putting them in the recycling bin. Got it. Check. Not exactly Mimi Miller material.

Why did I care? That's what Bee had asked. I don't know. Why did anyone in books care? Because there was a right, and a wrong, and people *should* care. *Be the change you wish to see in the world*—Mom had a T-shirt with that on it that she wore gardening. I would figure out why people didn't like Rachel, and I would make things right. Just like the heroes in my books were always doing. I didn't have any dragons to slay, but I did have a quest. Kind of.

I just didn't really know what to do next.

3

SEPTEMBER 16

To: LIST: Parents of East Eighth Graders

From: Principal Lila Howe <lhowe@east.middle.edu>

Subj: Fall Harvest Fest Fundraiser Invitation

Parents of East Middle School Eighth Graders,

You are cordially invited to the celebration of a lifetime—the
East Middle School eighth-grade Harvest Fest fundraiser!
Proceeds from this fundraiser will go toward important
eighth-grade events throughout the year, such as our winter
choral showcase and buses for our traveling sports teams.
Get excited for popcorn, cider, and fellowship with your
Knights family!

As per tradition, Harvest Fest will take place the first weekend in October. On Saturday, October 2, from 12:00–3:00 p.m., this family-friendly event will take place at the Eloise Event Center.

Due to the success of silent auctions in our past years, we've decided to charge forward with one this year. Some of our auction items include treasures such as:

- A wedding planning consultation with Lana McLeen, Wedding Queen
- A month's supply of bagels at Becker Bagel Co.
- A group Zumba class taught by ME, your very own princi-PAL!
  . . . and more!

Come dressed in your finest harvest wear, and let's celebrate our eighth graders! Especially after the unfortunate events surrounding the seventh-grade Spring Fling from last year, I know your eighth graders are looking forward to an event to remember. Please come ready to $upport our school! ;)

Best,
Lila Howe

SEPTEMBER 20

🌲:
Did you hear about the new girl?
Asking everyone about why nobody
likes Rachel Riley?

Cody:
Yeah . . . she seems weird.

🌲:
I don't know why she cares.

Cody:
Do u think she's actually
gonna find out?

🌲:
I don't know . . . that could be
pretty bad.

Cody:
Try REALLY bad.

SEPTEMBER 20

To: Lana McLeen <lana@lanamcleen.com>

From: Principal Lila Howe <lhowe@east.middle.edu>

Subj: Reminder of our cell phone policy

Lana,

I hope all is well and that you're eagerly preparing for next weekend's fundraiser activities! Unfortunately, I do feel the need to send you an email asking you to remind Cody about East's very strict cell phone policy. His phone was confiscated today during fifth period after two previous warnings. He also refused to say why he had his phone out or what he was using it for. He may collect his phone at the end of the day, but please remind him that the next time his phone is confiscated, it will result in a detention.

Best,

Lila Howe

SEPTEMBER 22

Bee:
Hey for the French hw are we supposed
to write a hobby we have or something
we want to learn how to do? Idk why
she gives the instructions IN FRENCH.
That's why we're taking the class lol

Anna:
Lol right? I think it's
something we want to
learn.

Bee:
Thanks. BTW . . . ru mad at me about last
week?

Anna:
About what??

Bee:
The RR thing

Anna:
I mean I know you told
everyone about my
podcast but it wasn't like
a secret. I'm just trying to
help her

Bee:
Honestly I'm telling you this because
you seem nice . . . what she did was
really low + she does not deserve your
help. If I was the new kid I would want
someone to tell me that

Anna:
So she did something that
made everyone mad??

Bee:
Yeah but idk I don't really like to talk
about it. It's kinda complicated. Just
ignore her that's what we all do

Anna:
I guess I just feel kinda
bad for her . . .

Bee:
Don't. 🙂

IT WAS ONE OF THOSE FIRST COLD DAYS, WHERE everyone realizes fall is coming but nobody remembers to grab a jacket on their way out the door. Nobody wanted to go outside after lunch, so most of us were squeezed into the library. Those With Friends were talking in fake whispers, Mr. Kim glancing over annoyed every few minutes and giving an exaggerated "shhh" like a librarian out of a TV show. Those Without Friends—Rachel and I—were bent over notebooks, halfheartedly trying to get homework done. Her table was on the other side of the library, and nobody was sitting within ten feet of her. It was like Social Outcast was a communicable disease.

I probably should have been working on my un-essay. I was planning on making some kind of scrapbook of collages from recycled materials. But it's not like I could go dumpster diving in the library. So instead, I tried to lay out what I had for my podcast so far.

Not much. I could feel Ira Glass and Mimi Miller shaking their heads at me.

Problem: Nobody wanted to talk about Rachel. Another problem: Rachel didn't want to talk to me herself. Even more problems: now that people knew I was working on the podcast, I couldn't really be undercover. All I had was confirmation that Rachel had *done* something, some *action*, that had been so treasonous the entire grade had turned against her. One measly text conversation with Bee—not exactly enough to solve a cold case.

Nice people can do crappy things. We all knew this. Kateri from youth group once stole a lip gloss from Target. I was all surprised when we got back to her house and she showed it to me, this bright pink shade she'd never in a million years wear. When I asked her why she stole it, she said she didn't know.

But what would make all of Rachel's friends completely turn their backs on her? I mean, if she'd *killed* someone, she'd be in jail, right? If she'd abused a puppy? Or broken into a house? What if I was trying to understand a girl who I shouldn't be able to understand? Trying to right a wrong that should just, well, stay a wrong?

Elizabeth Baker and Malika Jones were at the table next to me. They were the kind of best friends you started referring to as a pair: Elizabeth-and-Malika, Malika-and-Elizabeth. I knew that even though I'd barely been at East; that's how attached they were. Tied together, practically. You never saw one without the other. Elizabeth and Malika were girls with *causes*. They were the heads of Global Leaders, a club that raised money for nonprofits like the food bank, had speakers come in to educate students during assemblies, and brought awareness to social causes. So far at lunch, Malika and Elizabeth had asked me to sign petitions supporting refugee resettlement in Madison, a ban on fishermen from spear fishing year-round, and an end to smoking in any public park. Ms. O'Dell was their advisor.

As I was admitting podcast defeat and pulling out my algebra textbook, I noticed the gold glittery letters across the top of their poster. *Stop Trafficking Now.* I saw some of the statistics: *There are more people enslaved today than at any other time in human history. One in four victims of slavery are children. Eight hundred thousand people a year are trafficked across international borders.*

Malika caught me looking at them. "Hey. Are you interested in ending the plight of modern-day enslaved people?"

"Um." I cleared my throat. "I just thought your poster looked interesting."

"This isn't just an issue that affects developing nations," said Elizabeth, pointing a finger at me. Her nails were bright orange, dusted with the glitter they'd been using on their poster. "It takes place everywhere. Places you'd never think of. France, China, Norway, South Africa. The United States."

"Wow," I said. "I don't—I mean, I wouldn't really know how to help."

"It's about *spreading information*," said Malika. "Having hard conversations. Not just talking about the weather. Like, okay, it's cold today. Why do we all need to talk about it?" She had a point there.

Elizabeth pulled out a green flyer from her backpack, then reached over and put it on my table. "Come to Global Leaders sometime if you want. We're really trying to increase our reach this year."

"Thanks," I told her, picking the paper up and giving it a shake. "I'll . . . I'll see if I can make it."

They didn't look like they had too much hope. I wondered if Global Leaders had more than two members.

Maybe I *should* join Global Leaders, I thought. That'd probably be a more Mom-approved way of solving problems. It was an extracurricular. Good for college applications, which adults were already talking about even though we couldn't drive or get real jobs yet. But to be honest, people at East seemed to think Elizabeth-and-Malika were just as weird as my old classmates thought I was last year. I wasn't sure it would really help my nonexistent social status.

Suddenly—*slam*. Someone bumped into my chair—hard—shoving my stomach into the table.

"*Ouch,*" I yelped—too loudly. Mr. Kim turned to me so fast I thought he'd get whiplash. Blake Wyatt, the bumper, had his hands up, mouthing *sorry sorry sorry*. Satisfied, Mr. Kim turned back to lecturing some poor kid on the importance of finding their overdue *Captain Underpants* book.

"Dude, watch where you're *going,*" snickered Riz, who was right behind him, like always. Blake-and-Riz were another pair, but part of a larger group, too—Blake-and-Riz-and-Trevor-and-Carlos-and-Cody, all loud and usually wearing baggy East Middle or Green Bay Packers sweatshirts. Well, Cody had a Gandalf sweatshirt on the other day, but I think popular kids can get away with fantasy stuff in a way those of us lower on the scale can't. They were the ones who sat with Jordan Russell at lunch, the kind of guys who mimicked teachers when they turned their backs.

Nice enough, sometimes, but only if they liked you.

"Hey, you're the new girl," Riz said, plopping down at my table as if I'd invited him to pull up a chair.

I nodded. "Yeah. I'm Anna."

"Anna the detective, from what I've heard," Riz said. "Anna who sits by Rachel Riley at lunch. Anna, Banana, Fee-Fi-Fo-Fannah . . ."

"Rachel Riley," groaned Blake, making a face and sitting down. "What would you rather do, take her on a date or have to sit next to her in class every day till high school graduation?"

"Are you kidding me? Neither," said Riz, shaking his head.

"Hey, maybe she's a good kisser," said Blake. "Ask Cody."

"Cody? Tall blond guy?" I asked.

"Yeah, Sherlock," joked Blake. He looked surprised, like he'd forgotten I was even sitting there, two feet in front of him. "Tall blond guy." Riz burped, and Blake laughed. Mr. Kim gave them a loud *shhhh*.

"He says he's not friends with her anymore, but I know he is," Blake insisted in a loud whisper.

"Blake's a conspiracy theorist," said Riz. "He thinks they're keeping aliens locked up underneath the Capitol."

"I saw it in an article! I'm just saying."

"That time when you thought the janitor was a serial killer . . ."

"She looks just like that lady the one Facebook video was about!" He put his hands up. "But my cousin works at Lee's Dairy Emporium, and he said he's seen Cody and Rachel there together before. They're, like, totally dating."

"Friends, or dating?" I asked, glancing over at Rachel. She was writing in a notebook, completely oblivious.

"Um, *both*," said Blake. "Definitely." He made kissing noises, and Riz laughed and hit him on the shoulder. Blake hit him back. I felt like I was watching a documentary on cavemen or something. I saw Elizabeth glance at Malika and roll her eyes. They were clearly used to the obnoxiousness of Blake Wyatt and his friends.

Okay. So Cody was maybe Rachel's only friend? Then why didn't he sit with her at lunch? Why didn't he clap for her on her birthday? Why was he hanging out with her at Lee's Dairy Emporium, but not ever in the hallways? And if what Blake said was true, why was Cody trying to keep it a secret from his friends?

The bell rang. Elizabeth-and-Malika packed up their poster and art supplies, and other kids shoved their math textbooks into their backpacks. I wondered how Elizabeth-and-Malika had the energy in them to save the world. I was trying to help one girl's reputation *maybe* get fixed, and it was exhausting. Not only did I have little to no concrete evidence of what had turned Rachel Riley into a friendless pariah, but now I had secondhand reports of a boyfriend. A *popular* boyfriend.

This is the part they leave out, in focused attempts at justice: that you will occasionally want to push it all aside and curl up for one big nap instead.

4

SEPTEMBER 26

To: Sierra Kincaid <skincaid@kincaidfarms.com>
From: Principal Lila Howe <lhowe@east.middle.edu>
Subj: GREAT news!!!

Sierra,

I'm writing to truly, deeply, passionately apologize for my last email. It was much too harsh and I wrote it out of a place of emotion. Say you'll forgive me?

As a celebration of our reconciled friendship, I have some good news for you—the Eloise Event Center has canceled our Harvest Fest fundraiser this weekend due to a burst pipe! That means East Middle School will instead be hosting our annual gala at *your* beautiful new event space. We'll need seating for five hundred, overflow parking, an AV system, and some of those gigantic space heaters—the first weekend of October is always so chilly! I know you said you weren't technically reopening until the following weekend, but for such a dear friend, I hope you'll make an exception.

I'll be there on Friday at 6:00 p.m. to walk you through our design plans.

See you in Zumba!

Your friend,
Lila Howe

SEPTEMBER 27

To: Sierra Kincaid <skincaid@kincaidfarms.com>

From: Principal Lila Howe <lhowe@east.middle.edu>

Subj: Re: re: GREAT news!!!

Sierra,

The first requested document is attached. Will be forwarding the second one ASAP.

Regards,
Lila Howe

East Middle School formally accepts responsibility for any vandalism that takes place at the Kincaid Farms Event Barn, including any damage done by fire, graffiti, or insubordinate preteens.

*_X_* Lila Howe

SEPTEMBER 27

To: Kristy Riley <kristy.riley@rileygraphics.com>
From: Principal Lila Howe <lhowe@east.middle.edu>
Subj: Rachel's attendance at Harvest Fest

Kristy,

I hope all is well with you and your lovely family. I recently spoke to Mr. Selefah about Rachel's extra violin rehearsals, and he said she's one of the most promising music students he's ever had the good fortune to teach!

Unfortunately, I have some news that may be somewhat upsetting. Eloise Event Center has had to cancel our Harvest Fest last-minute due to a pipe situation, and unfortunately, our only available option is to celebrate our festival in the newly rebuilt Kincaid Farms Event Barn. As I'm sure you understand, the Kincaid family is hesitant about allowing your daughter on their property.

Sierra Kincaid has specifically requested that you fill out the attached waiver, which will accept financial consequences for any damage done to the barn by Rachel.

Best,
Lila Howe

SEPTEMBER 28

To: Principal Lila Howe <lhowe@east.middle.edu>
From: Kristy Riley <kristy.riley@rileygraphics.com>
Subj: RE: Rachel's attendance at Harvest Fest

Lila,

As we both know, there's more to the story of what happened at the dairy barn last year. And while I'm not sure what that story *is*, I know my daughter. I'm disappointed with this continued narrative that she is some kind of teenage felon.

I will not be filling out the requested form, as our family has decided to skip Harvest Fest this year.

Sincerely,
Kristy

SEPTEMBER 29

Anna: This is WHAT HAPPENED TO RACHEL RILEY?: AN INVESTIGATION BY ANNA HUNT.

Cody: You sound kind of like the girl who does SERIAL.

Anna: Oh my gosh—thanks. That's exactly what I'm going for. Anyway. Thanks for talking to me.

<sound of basketball bouncing>

Cody: I mean, I didn't really agree to talk to you. I'm at the park trying to shoot hoops and you're sticking a phone in my face.

Anna: Well . . . whatever. I have it on good authority that you're still friends with Rachel Riley.

Cody: Good authority? You mean Blake?

Anna: I can't reveal my sources.

Cody: Yeah, well, Blake is always making that garbage up. I'm not friends with her.

Anna: But then why would he say that?

Cody: I don't know. He's a liar.

Anna: He's your friend.

<sound of basketball swishing through hoop>

Cody: And a liar.

Anna: So you unequivocally deny any association with the mentioned party?

Cody: Huh?

Anna: You're not friends with her?

Cody: No. I'm not. And you're weirding me out. So . . . just leave me alone.

Anna: But—

Cody: Bye, Hannah.

Anna: It's Anna.

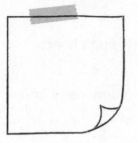

SEPTEMBER 29

Jordan—

What ru wearing to Harvest Fest this weekend?
I'm thinking my new skinny jeans with my sister's ankle
booties . . . if she'll let me steal them. Idk it might be too
muddy! Is putting my hair in braids too cowgirl?

Xoxo

Kaylee

Kaylee—

Your hair would be so cute in braids!!! I love that idea.
And if Jenna doesn't let you steal her shoes, you can borrow
mine?? I'm a size 6. I'm gonna wear my riding boots I think,
and my red and silver flannel. And I think all the dance team
girls are doing red ribbons in our hair. Do you want to come
over and get ready first and then ride with my family?

OxOx

Jordan

Jordan—

Yes! I may be tired though haha, I have Nutcracker auditions the night before. Eeeeeek.

Xoxo

Kaylee

Kaylee—

You will KILL IT! Do you think we should invite Anna, too?? She seems kind of nice. I know the Rachel project thing is weird but maybe if we became her friends she'd leave us out of it . . . is that too Undercover Agent? Lol.

OxOx

Jordan

Jordan—

Idk . . . let's keep it just us. I don't like the way she's always asking questions.

Xoxo

Kaylee

SEPTEMBER 30

To: Katarzyna Kowalski <babciakat@gmail.com>
From: Anna Hunt <ahunt@east.middle.edu>
Subj: Re: Re: new email

Babcia,

Haha! I love what you wrote about what you used to bring to school for lunch in Poland. I know, I know . . . I shouldn't be complaining as long as I have food to eat. That's wild that the stores had no meat during communism! But carp?! Blech.

This weekend I'm going to Harvest Fest. It's, like, this big fundraiser party thing that our school has every year. We raise money for things like buses to take our basketball teams to away games. I don't really want to go, but my parents are still on me about "making new friends." I told them I *have* friends—I have you, and you're my best friend. But they said eighty-year-olds don't count. Sorry.

Here's the thing, Babcia. Us girls are told to speak our minds and be all that we can be. Glass ceilings, buh-bye, right?! Tough girls in superhero capes. But . . . eighth grade just isn't like that. Most girls I know have some kind of girl-power quote in their Instagram bio but still won't answer a question in history even if they know the answer because they don't want to look like a nerd. Or you can answer *one* question, but not two or three. Everything is, like, a calculation, or a game you play in gym class, one with rules and regulations. You probably don't like hearing this. You probably thought that we would all be different, right? Because we have a female vice president and plus-sized models can be on magazine covers. I'm not fighting the communists in Poland. But when you're in gym class and none of the girls want to play volleyball too hard in case they start sweating, it doesn't feel that much different.

Anyway, Nik is making friends. Nikola! My weird sister, who never left her room in Chicago and spent all of her time making apps and playing games about aliens on her computer. She's gone to the movies a few times and to get ice cream. She joined some kind of club at the high school that mentors elementary schoolers on coding. *My* sister—it's wild, right? And she has a boy who texts her all the time, too. She told me about him.

I love that you want to hear penguin facts. All right, here's the first one: there are twenty-eight species of penguins. Can you name any of them?

That's all that's new with us. I miss you lots + lots + lots.

Love,
Anna

"LET ME SEE," I WHINED. I HAD JUST POPPED INTO Nik's room and she was sitting at her desk, glued to her phone. I *knew* she was texting that boy—she'd shown me his picture and everything. Bronson Webb. He had black curly hair, and it fell in his eyes. He was always posting Instagram pictures of his guitar.

"No," she said, rolling her eyes. "Get out of here." Sisters. Yesterday, she'd divulged how he called her Nikki, the only person in the world who ever did that, while we watched old episodes of *Umbrella Academy*. Today, she wanted me to stay fifteen feet away from her at all times.

"I have to get ready for this Harvest Fest thing. Do you have any flannel? We're supposed to dress . . . harvest-y."

"What does that mean?"

"Like farmers? I don't know."

"Um, I might. Check my closet. A blue one, maybe."

Nik didn't have many clothes in her closet. It was basically a compartment for all of her extra cords

75

and cables. So it was easy to find the blue flannel, all plaid and cozy and oversized. My favorite kind of shirt. I pulled it on and looked in the mirror. I guess I was harvest-y.

"Anna Maria! Two minutes," Mom called up the stairs. I heard her pouring food into the dogs' bowls and the happy click-clickity-click of their nails on the kitchen floor.

"Go," said Nik, swatting her hand like I was a fly.

"Thanks for the shirt."

"Farmer chic. Ha."

I crawled into the back of the Camry, in my usual seat behind Dad. Mom glanced at me through the rearview mirror. "I'm excited to meet some of your new classmates today."

I shrugged, looking out the window. Kincaid Farms was in an area I'd never been to—not far outside Madison, but far enough that the houses were getting farther and farther apart, and we were starting to see barns and fields of corn. Cows, too, looking bored and dusty.

"Do you think that Rachel girl will be there?" Dad asked.

"I don't know," I said. "I mean, it sounds like everyone is going . . . but I don't really know who she'd hang out with or anything." I didn't know who *I* was going to hang out with. But Harvest Fest seemed like a thing everyone went to, and my parents wanted to go show their support for the school. So there I was, in my too-big flannel and messy ponytail, ready for Operation Be Normal.

"I'm glad you decided against that project," Mom said as she checked her blind spot.

"I didn't 'decide against it.' Ms. O'Dell wouldn't let me do it." I hadn't told Mom and Dad about the podcast I was making. Sitting through a *stop being nosy and make some friends* lecture sounded boring. Besides, *if* I got into the summer program, they might not even let me go. No sense in rocking the parental boat before all my plans were lined up.

We drove under a huge arched sign that read *Kincaid Farms*. There were multiple barns—one that looked like a real barn, with cows, and one that looked like the kind of place you have weddings. There was a sign with an arrow pointing toward another sign that said *East Middle School Harvest Fest*.

Mom pulled the car into the overflow parking lot, and we trekked across the bumpy field to the event barn. It looked new and smelled like fresh paint.

"Welcome, welcome!" Principal Howe stood at the entrance, waving to all of the families as they strolled in. "Make sure to take a look at our silent auction table, buy tickets for our carnival games, and support *your* East Middle School Knights!"

I had that urge you get when you're in a crowded space to cling to the people you know. I saw a bunch of kids—Kaylee and Jordan and Blake and others—but I stayed glued to my parents' side. There were lots of other grown-ups, obviously parents, holding little plastic cups of cider and laughing loudly.

"Auction stuff," said Mom, nodding toward the long tables. "We were supposed to donate something, but—what? A criminal defense?"

"You're not even that kind of lawyer," I said with an eye roll.

"Tuition at UW," Dad joked. "That would have gone in a flash."

"Could have paid for every bus for ten years," said Mom. "Anna, why don't you go find some of your friends?"

I wished Bee was there, at least, but I didn't see her yet. Kaylee and Jordan had tucked in the fronts of their flannel shirts, letting the backs hang down over their butts. I wished I'd thought to do that. I couldn't fix it now, or I would look like I was copying them. But wait—weren't we supposed to look like farmers? I looked more ready to shovel manure than they did.

It was either go talk to the other kids or have Mom

78

lecture me about the importance of social interaction for the rest of the weekend, so I just nodded and took off in the direction of the concession stand. With popcorn in my hand, I could probably work up the courage to talk to people. I still felt like everywhere I went, people were looking, whispering, wondering.

The woman behind the concession stand looked like a parent volunteer—a denim skirt and a flannel shirt, complete with a cowboy hat. I didn't think farmers wore cowboy hats, but whatever. She had on high-heeled boots, too. She'd probably done a front-tuck of her shirts when she was in eighth grade.

"Welcome to Harvest Fest! What can I get for you, dear?" she asked.

"Um . . . popcorn, please."

"Anna!" I turned to see Bee, and I was thankful-thankful-thankful. The one person I kind-of-sort-of talked to.

"Hey," I said. "Just . . . getting something to munch."

"Come on outside. That's where the games and stuff are. I mean, not that we're playing any, but that's where everyone is."

"Everyone," I soon learned, was the popular group: Kaylee and Jordan and Blake and Riz, all standing in a circle and talking. Bee was kind of like, well, a bee:

it was like she could buzz around all these different groups, just being nice and fitting in. Elizabeth-and-Malika were there, too, looking like they were actually having fun, trying to shoot a ball through a small hoop for a carnival game instead of thinking about flash floods or child poverty. Other kids were standing around, rubbing their arms to keep warm.

"Look, just play it cool about the Rachel thing, okay?" Bee said under her breath as we approached the group. "They don't really like to talk about it."

Blake and Riz weren't exactly who I would have chosen to spend my free time with, but Bee was my only option, and that's where she was headed. I thought of Rachel, reading *Wonder* at lunch. This was exactly the kind of moment where I'd rather be reading a book.

"Is she here? Or coming? Rachel, I mean," I asked Bee. She snatched my elbow, hard. We were still a good seven feet or so away from the group.

"*No.* She's not even allowed on the premises, I heard," hissed Bee.

"*What?*" Harvest Fest was to make money, wasn't it? If your parents were willing to buy you popcorn and bid on a pair of earrings made from porcupine quills, weren't you allowed in? *Allowed on the premises.* It sounded like something my mom would say, in her lawyer shoes, standing in front of a lecture hall.

She grabbed her braid and started nibbling on the end. "We don't like to talk about it," she repeated. "Nobody does. It's all over, anyway, so we're just . . . moving on. Without Rachel."

"Talk about *what*?" I asked. "Can't you at least tell me—"

"Are you two coming over here, or what?" called out Kaylee.

Bee and I looked at each other, having an entire silent conversation. My eyes asked her to tell me why Rachel wasn't at Harvest Fest. Her eyes asked me to shut the heck up—politely.

"Hi, Anna," said Jordan, as Bee and I joined the group. She was nice. Jordan was the kind of person who was nice to *everyone*, which made me like her. She was Amanda Bennett's lab partner, and I may have been the new kid, but it didn't take a month to learn Amanda Bennett always smelled like soup and wore these bright woolen sweaters. But I'd look over during science and see the two of them giggling together.

"Ooh, nice popcorn, Anna. Thanks," said Blake. He reached over and took a handful. I felt weird, suddenly, about having food. Nobody else did. Blake shoved the kernels in his mouth, and a few fell to the ground. Jordan, Bee, and Kaylee laughed, so I did, too.

"Where's Cody?" Bee asked. "I saw his mom in there. Every time I see her, her hair is bigger."

"Sick, quote unquote," said Riz. "I think he just didn't want to stand out here in the cold like the rest of us suckers."

"Or watch his mom do the auctioneering," snickered Kaylee.

"Cody's mom is Lana McLeen," Bee whispered to me. Lana McLeen, Wedding Queen had a billboard we passed every day on the way to school, where she was pointing some kind of magic fairy wand toward a beautiful blushing bride.

I stood there for a half hour, willing myself to talk about TikTok and kids I didn't know and how cold it was. But finally I surrendered and went back in to find my parents.

"Were those kids your new friends?" Mom whispered as I slid into the seat next to hers. The barn was set up with huge tables, each one covered by tablecloths with the Knights logo printed all over them. Dad was talking to another parent about the Packers. At the front of the barn was a stage where a photo slideshow was playing, showing pictures of kids in East Middle School T-shirts.

I nodded.

"You can keep hanging out with them, if you want!" she said. "Don't feel like you need to hang out with your boring parental units." I felt bad. She looked so excited at the prospect of *new friends*. But I was kind of annoyed, too. Didn't she want me around?

"I was cold," I said. The truth was more like *bored*. I should have snuck a book into my bag. But I guess sitting there reading wouldn't have exactly screamed *Trying To Make Friends*.

The rest of the afternoon went by quickly. Mom and I played Guess What That Person Does For a Living, which is one of our favorite games in big crowds of people. Then she guilt-bought a Kate Spade purse even though she wasn't the type to carry a Kate Spade purse—her satchel from Target was always getting stained with coffee. After another hour, Dad checked his phone and did the customary grown-up move of slapping his knees and saying, "Well, shall we?"

As we walked out, Mom chatted with Lana McLeen, the Wedding Queen herself. Shuffling toward the exit, I heard Lana mention to my mom she had her first wedding at the barn next weekend.

"It's new, huh?" Mom asked, looking around. "Smells new, that's for sure."

"Oh yes," said Lana. "The old one . . . well, there

was an incident last year. It burned down. Quite unfortunate."

And as we drove home in our car, Kenny Chesney singing about his tractor on the radio and Mom talking about all the papers she needed to grade, I remembered what Bee said about Rachel and the barn: *not even allowed on the premises*.

A fire.

This, I believed, was what Mimi Miller would call *a lead*.

WISCONSIN STATE JOURNAL

JUNE 5, 2021
ACCESSED OCTOBER 3

Madison firefighters battled a fire that broke out at the Kincaid Farms Event Barn on Agriculture Road early Saturday morning. The fire was unintentionally set by a minor who had been trespassing on the property, fire department spokesman Joel Andetti said.

Firefighters were notified of the fire at approximately 12:14 a.m. and arrived six minutes later. The building contained no additional people. The minor was unharmed but brought to Meriter Hospital to be evaluated for exposure to smoke.

The Madison Police Department had no comment regarding if the minor would face charges as the incident is still under investigation.

Kincaid Farms has been a staple in Madison for decades. The Event Barn was constructed in 1985 and has since hosted corporate gatherings, weddings, and other celebrations. The barn was reportedly going to hold a dance and awards ceremony for East Middle School's seventh graders Saturday night. The event has since been canceled.

OCTOBER 3

🌲:
Why weren't you at Harvest Fest?

Cody:
I felt weird! Idk.
Everything is so different
this year

🌲:
Bc of what happened last year?

Cody:
The barn fire? Yeah

🌲:
And the other stuff too

Cody:
Yeah. The other stuff too.

OCTOBER 5

To: LIST: Parents of East Eighth Graders

From: Principal Lila Howe <lhowe@east.middle.edu>

Subj: THANK YOU!

Parents of East Middle School Eighth Graders,

THANK YOU! You made this year's Harvest Fest the BEST YET. We managed to raise enough money for this grade's winter and spring extracurriculars and activities as needed.

Here at East, we value a collaborative environment and welcome all suggestions from the parents that make our school so terrific. We received numerous requests for a portion of the money raised to be used for a winter dance. In light of the cancellation of this particular class's seventh-grade Spring Fling, we understand that there's a desire for some sort of celebration and social event to make up for it. This has been put under consideration by your East Middle admin team!

There were also suggestions for next year's Harvest Fest to include more gluten-free, keto, and paleo snack options. I assure you we will be more aware of allergies and food sensitivities in the future.

Last, we received numerous notes about our decision to host the festival at a corporate dairy barn in a time when we know what we know about factory farms. Rest assured, Kincaid Farms is an exceptional institution that only treats their cows with the highest degree of respect.

Moooo-ve over, summer—here comes AUTUMN!

Best,
Lila Howe

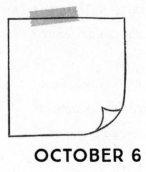

OCTOBER 6

Anna—

Just a reminder that Global Leaders meets today after school and we'd love to have you. We're talking about the backlash to Harvest Fest being held at Kincaid Farms and the way that dairy farms are basically RUINING the entire planet!!! Ugh. You seem like you care about that kind of stuff . . . so maybe we'll see you there!

Elizabeth

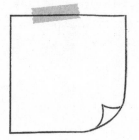

Mrs. Cleary,

I'm very sorry for writing notes during class.
However, I would like to share with you that cow
manure contributes to greenhouse gas emissions and
is a major problem affecting our environment. If
Earth gets ruined and we all die, nobody's going to
need to understand sentence structure.

—Elizabeth M. Baker

OCTOBER 7

Anna: This is WHAT HAPPENED TO RACHEL RILEY?: AN INVESTIGATION BY ANNA HUNT. *I'm speaking with Rachel Riley herself.*

Rachel: I told you I wasn't going to help you.

Anna: Can you say that right into the phone, please?

Rachel: <louder> I said I wasn't going to help you with your podcast application.

Anna: How did you know it's for an application?

Rachel: Because you told Bee. Are you kidding me? That girl couldn't keep a secret even if it meant getting free Billie Eilish tickets. These days, if I hear a secret she's spilling, you can be guaranteed the entire school already knows. Now leave me alone. I'm trying to read.

Anna: I've been doing some research involving an incident that occurred near the end of last school year. Do you know which incident I'm referring to?

Rachel: The day a racoon got stuck in the dumpster

and Coach Watt had to bribe it with Reese's Puffs cereal to come out?

Anna: No.

Rachel: The day Principal Howe wore a bright orange jumpsuit to school and everyone started calling her "Orange Is the New Principal"?

Anna: Are you messing with me?

Rachel: Why don't you just ask me what you really want to know?

Anna: Do you confirm or deny that you were the minor who set the Kincaid Farms barn on fire?

<silence>

<silence>

<silence>

Anna: Do you need me to repeat the question?

Rachel: No.

Anna: No, you don't need me to repeat the question, or no, you can't confirm or deny?

Rachel: No, I don't need you to repeat the question, and no, I can't deny.

Anna: So—wait. So you confirm?

Rachel: I'm reading.

Anna: But . . . why? Why did you do it? The article said it was unintentional. But what were you doing there at midnight? And how do you, like, unintentionally set a barn on fire?

Rachel: Answering those questions would be called "helping," which I told you I'm not doing. Why do you think anyone would even be interested in this?

Anna: . . . I am.

Rachel: What?

Anna: I'm interested. I see you here, every day, by yourself, just reading. With no friends. No one clapping on your birthday. No one talking to you in the halls. And I care. I don't think . . . I don't think someone should have to live like that, in eighth grade. I know what it's like to be lonely. That's all.

<silence>

<silence>

<silence>

Rachel: You're too nice for this school, Anna.

Anna: But—

Rachel: I'm reading now. For real, okay?

EVER SINCE WE MOVED TO WISCONSIN, I HAVEN'T been a great sleeper. In spite of all its sirens and honking and drunk people walking down the street in the middle of the night, I was used to Chicago— its noise. Its *business*. I also shared a room with Nik there, and the hum of her eighty-seven million computer screens was kind of like a white noise machine. She snored, too, though she'd never admit it. And not little ladylike snores, either. It was a lawn mower situation. Mom even got her tested for sleep apnea once.

They thought I'd be so happy to have my own room in Madison. It was one of the big perks of moving, they kept reminding us. A house, with a backyard, and four whole bedrooms. And I *was* happy, at first. I hung up these cool pink-and-gray prints from Hobby Lobby and a giant Polish flag. No annoying computer hum.

But it was *quiet*, without that hum. Without any of Nik's Sleeping Sounds.

It was dark, too. Dark house after dark house, and

our street didn't even have streetlights. A big, endless dark sky, with a small smattering of stars. No corner store just across the street, with its giant sign offering a deal on hot dogs lit at all hours of the night. No blinking red light on Nik's laptop. But what, like I was supposed to get a night-light? I'm thirteen.

Anyway, for all those reasons and more, I couldn't sleep at night. I tossed and turned, thinking about fires and barns and Rachel Riley. And what Rachel said about nobody being interested. *I* was. *I* cared.

I'd always been someone who cared. A box of puppies on the street in Chicago—I'd think about them all day, wondering what was going to happen to them. The homeless people who lived under the bridge, who we'd walk past whenever we went down to the lakeshore. I cared *too* much, sometimes, and that was part of why I probably didn't have a ton of friends. I wasn't Elizabeth-and-Malika level, trying to end carbon emissions worldwide, but there *were* things that I really cared about. The K wing at my old school was where special education classes were held, and kids called the students that had class there "Special K kids." That always bugged me, and I'd say so, and they'd just roll their eyes at me. That sort of thing. I'd stay up late at night, too, with thoughts running through my head. I hated feeling like bad things were going on all around me and I couldn't do anything about it. It was hard for me to actually have fun with other groups of kids—I guess I just felt like what we talked about was stupid and pointless. Or I'd be enjoying myself, and then I'd remember someone's face that I saw on the news, and all night, they'd be all I could think about.

So when we moved here, Mom talked to me about the importance of fitting in. Not trying to fix everything. But things could always be fixed. Sabrina, my lab partner back in Chicago, had at least stopped calling Morgan D'Angelo "Special K." Isn't that what adults were always telling us to do? Use our voice. Make a difference. *Yes*, Mom had said. *But also, be strategic. You can't get through life intimidating the crap out of everybody.* Sabrina had stopped being kinda-sorta-friendly to me after I'd called her out. But who cared? I had Tris Prior, and Yumi Chung. The girls from my books made more sense to me than anyone at school.

So I was trying. I was! I'd chosen Rachel Riley for my podcasting summit application, and maybe that was kind of in-your-face. But Bee and I texted about homework, sometimes. Kaylee Nakamura had lent me her pen when mine ran out of ink. If we weren't friends, we were at least *friendly*.

You're too nice for this school, Rachel had said. But I wasn't all that nice, really. There was a difference between caring and *nice*. I bugged Nik a lot, just because I could. I thought mean things, too, about Blake Wyatt and Riz Kapoor and the rest of them. Mean, *I'm nicer than you* things. Thinking *I'm nicer than you* kind of automatically makes you not that nice. I was also ignoring Elizabeth-and-Malika's attempts to get me to join Global Leaders, because I was too busy with my own podcast to help them make posters or organize bake sales. Besides, for all their poster-making and money-raising, it didn't really seem like they'd made any kind of *impact*. Not like Mimi Miller talked about.

I just didn't get *why*. Why would Rachel burn down the barn? Why would everyone else be so mad, so furious with her that they completely cut her out of their lives? A dance—so what? Just a bunch of music in a gym. Just a bowl of punch and bored-looking art teachers. And why would everyone refuse to talk about it? Did other people do something mean to Rachel first? Meaner than sabotaging a dance with a *fire*?

I kept picking up pieces and trying to make them fit, jamming them in like a puzzle. Turning them this way and that, the way you do when you've got the edge pieces down and are trying to figure out the middle. But none of it clicked.

I glanced at my phone—9:35, I heard Mom knock on Nik's door and remind her not to stay up too late before going to bed. 10:00, I heard Dad join Mom. 11:12, finally, Nik's light clicked off and I heard her crawl into her own bed across her squeaky bedroom floor. 12:35, I could hear Kix the night owl wandering around the kitchen before getting comfy in his own bed. 1:12. 2:15.

It was 2:40 before I got out of bed, dragging my pillow and the green quilt Babcia had made me when I was in preschool. I tiptoed, soft as I could, to Nik's room. Her door made a creaking noise as I nudged it open, but she didn't wake up. I was surprised I could even hear it, over the orchestra that was Nik's Sleeping Sounds.

I lay down next to her bed on her soft blue rug, pulled my quilt up to my chin, and finally, finally, finally fell asleep.

6

YOU'RE INVITED

What: Bee Becker's 14th Birthday Party

Where: 205 Winnequah Road

When: Friday, October 15, at 8:00 PM

Anna—we have a hot tub,
so bring your swimsuit!
Hope you can make it.

OCTOBER 13

To: Katarzyna Kowalski <babciakat@gmail.com>

From: Anna Hunt <ahunt@east.middle.edu>

Subj: Good things <3

Babcia,

I'm sorry my email made you sad. You're right, eighth grade just doesn't change that much through the years.

But don't be sad. There's a lot of good things happening in Madison, too. Like:

I think Mom really likes teaching at UW. She works a lot, but her smiles meet her eyes most of the time.

Kix and Jesse have a yard now, so Kix is less hyper.

Remember that time you were visiting and he scratched a hole through the wall in our Chicago apartment? You could see the pipes and everything.

I'm working on Being Social and Making Friends, Mom's big hope for me. I got invited to a girl's house this weekend for her birthday party. I think she invited every girl in the class, but whatever. Actually, that isn't true . . . I don't think Rachel was invited.

Classes aren't that hard, and I barely have any homework. The teachers are pretty nice. And I like not having to wear a uniform. My St. Patrick's skirt was always so itchy.
I think Nik is a lot happier here in Madison.

You asked if we had a Polish grocery store here, and the answer is no. Mom said one of these weekends we can go to Milwaukee, where they have one. I'm desperate for some *ptasie mleczko*. I wouldn't mind going to our old Polish church, either. Some days, I just want to be surrounded by all of those clunky words. I could forget I was Polish, here. There are some kids from different countries at my school, or who can speak other languages, but it's mostly Spanish or Mandarin. Chicago had such a big Polish community that I could feel like I was in Poland, even in America. I miss it a lot.

And the penguins—good job! You got the emperor, the Australian, the Humboldt, and the Adélie penguins, but you forgot the African, the northern rockhopper, the eastern rockhopper, the southern rockhopper, the king, the allied king, the fairy, the yellow-eyed, the chinstrap, the Magellanic, the macaroni, the Snares, Galapagos, the erect-crested, the royal, the Fiordland, the Falkland Islands, the Kerguelen, the Gentoo, the South Georgia, the white-flippered, the Cook Strait, the Chatham Island, and the Kairuku penguins.

Okay, next question . . . Can you figure out who the most famous penguin researcher is?

I miss you.

Love,
Anna

OCTOBER 13

Anna:
Hey do u know where
Dad is? Just got home
from school and he's not
here + not answering his
phone

Nik:
He had a meeting like down on campus
I think

Anna:
Oh ok gotchya

Nik:
BTW I'm with some girls right now at
CodeHERs and they're talking about
your school

Anna:
lol what? What about it

Nik:
Do you know what the game is? Lol
they're being dumb they won't tell me

Anna:
Which game?

Nik:
Idk they're just calling it "the game"

Anna:
No clue

Nik:
They said a bunch of guys played it
there last year and now they brought
it here but they won't tell me what it is.
Probably something dumb

Anna:
Lol prob. Will you be
home for dinner

Nik:
Yeah I think so

OCTOBER 13

This is Anna Hunt, reporting for WHAT HAPPENED TO RACHEL RILEY? *Now that I've discovered that Rachel burned down the Kincaid Farms Event Barn, you'd think I'd be done with my research. But the truth is, this answer just brings up more questions.*

Here are some of the ones I'm thinking about:

Why did Rachel burn down the barn?

If it was an accident, why are the other kids so mad?

Was it an accident? If it was, what was she doing in the barn in the middle of the night in the first place?

Since Rachel burned down the barn, the seventh-grade dance was canceled. I get it . . . They only get one, and it was a really big deal. Plus, they did awards, too—like, ones for subjects, like whoever was the best at math or writing. I found some old yearbooks in the library, and they all have an entire page dedicated to the seventh-grade dance and awards ceremony. There was also the Rose Award, which is basically given to whoever the kindest person was. And so people were really, really upset the dance got canceled. But . . . the reaction just seems a bit extreme.

Anyway. I have more questions than answers at this point. But it seems like all important issues in life don't have cut-and-dried answers. I mean, if world hunger could be solved with a policy, we'd do it, right? Things have pros and cons. Shades of gray. One person's truth and another person's truth colliding— and that may turn into the truth, or it may turn into a bunch of different perspectives all arguing with each other.

This has been Anna Hunt. Over and out.

DAD FINALLY GOT HOME, LOOKING EXHAUSTED.

"Long meeting?" I asked him as he pulled a Tupperware out of the fridge. He lifted the tinfoil covering it and gave it a sniff.

"How do you feel about Chinese food?" he asked.

"Very positively," I said.

"I need something . . . filling, you know? And hot. That comes in a white Styrofoam container," he said.

"Cashew chicken, please."

He grabbed his phone from his pocket and pulled up DoorDash. "And yes, the meeting was long. Work is . . . oof. It's hard work, kid. Enjoy your days of freedom."

I rolled my eyes. "You work from the living room in your sweatpants most days, and I have to go to a brick building and be lectured on the different types of plants found in Wisconsin prairies."

He didn't look up from his phone. "Do you think two things of crab rangoons? Three? Will your sister be home? Anyway, listen, at least you get to switch topics every hour. I have to talk about mergers all day, every day."

"I texted her, but she said she didn't know. Just get three." The more crab rangoons, the better, in the official Hunt Family Opinion.

Kix trotted up to my feet and whined, so I bent down and scratched behind his ear. Jesse stared on jealously.

"Did your mom just pull in?" Dad asked, glancing up. "Thought I heard a car door."

I looked out into the driveway and saw Mom, but she was talking to Mrs. Boyd, who was pregnant and lived right next door. The two of them were always chatting. You wouldn't really think they had much in common—Mrs. Boyd was young, probably only in her twenties, and she stayed home all day with her sticky toddler, Cooper. They did those mommy-and-me classes where everyone sits around and bangs on a drum. Mom wouldn't have been caught dead in one of those. I'm pretty sure I went to day care at, like, four weeks old. But they liked each other.

"She's talking to Mrs. Boyd," I reported back.

Dad rolled his eyes. "They'll be out there awhile. Hey, grab me a beer from the fridge, would you? Then come tell your poor old man about eighth grade."

I reached into the fridge and tossed him a cold

bottle, which he expertly caught. He leaned over and opened it on the kitchen counter, his special trick. I slid onto a stool at the breakfast bar.

"It's fine," I said. "Mostly. I got invited to a birthday party."

"Oh, really? That's fun."

"Yeah, a girl in my French class."

"Not the girl you wanted to do the big project on."

"No," I said, shaking my head. "I think if she had a birthday party, the guest list would be zero."

"Poor kid," Dad said.

I opened my mouth. Shut it. Opened it again. Shut it again. I didn't know—what if I told my parents Rachel burned down the barn and they sided with the other kids? What if they thought she was some kind of arson pyromaniac? I knew there was more to the story than that—there had to be. I wasn't sure I was ready to open Rachel up to their judgments along with everyone else's. And I definitely wasn't ready to tell them about my project for Mimi Miller.

"What *are* you doing your project on?"

Before I could admit that I hadn't even started my recycling scrapbook, the front door banged open, and in came Mom, looking tired.

"Husband, daughter number two—I'm starving," Mom said. "Tell me we have a plan for dinner."

"Ming's China Palace," Dad responded.

"Did you get two things of crab rangoons or three?"

Mothers: they know us, and we know them, whether we like it or not.

I didn't have a clue what to get Bee Becker. It's not like I knew her very well outside of French class, besides that long blonde braid and her collection of sparkly gel pens. But she'd been friendly to me so far this year, and I wanted to get her something she'd like. It didn't seem like she played a sport, and she'd never mentioned being in any clubs or anything. She had a BTS binder, but everyone had a BTS binder.

Anyway, I figured I'd get her a book. It seemed harmless. Who doesn't like to read? Well, there's where I went wrong—a lot of people don't like to read. But *I* liked to read, and Nik liked to read, and Rachel Riley liked to read, so I got her *Song for a Whale* by Lynne Kelly, one of my favorite books of all time, about a girl who is deaf who ends up helping an abandoned whale. Dad wrapped it for me in some of our leftover Christmas wrapping paper from last year, and I hoped she didn't mind the candy canes.

But when Nik dropped me off at Bee's, I felt dumb almost right away. Just that sense of *not belonging* that I always felt around other people. I wasn't exactly an expert birthday party attendee, unless you count elementary school, where kids invited the whole class to places like Trampoline World or the pet store. The party was down in her basement, which was massive. There were huge gold balloons spelling out *Happy Birthday Bee* and a table filled with yummy-looking treats that nobody was eating. There was a hot tub, and it was already packed with people—I'd brought my suit, but it was my navy-blue one piece I'd worn at the YMCA in Chicago. These girls were in, like, real bikinis, the kind for people with real curves. Okay, real *boobs*, of which I had none. Kaylee and Jordan were in there, and so were Carmen Gomez and Lia Lipton, who spent all of gym class complaining about their periods so they didn't have to do anything. I didn't even *have* my period. Yeah, I was a year younger than almost everyone in our class, but still—I felt like such a little kid around everybody.

Bee was there, too, obviously. She was holding a bottle of water and laughing at something a girl I didn't know was saying. I gave her a little half wave, but she didn't see me.

"Anna!" Jordan was waving me over. I walked to the hot tub and just stood there awkwardly, clutching my candy-cane wrapping paper, my little-kid swimsuit shoved in my North Face pocket.

"Change and get in," said Jordan. "It feels amazing." Jordan Russell was the kind of person who saw you were alone at a party and didn't want you to be alone at a party, you know? Just *friendly*.

"Um . . . I forgot my suit," I lied.

"Oh no!" said Jordan. "I'm sure Bee has one you can borrow. Bee!" Before I could stop her, she was yelling Bee over, who trotted to the tub, eyes shining and happy.

"Anna forgot her suit," said Jordan.

"Oh my gosh. No problem. We have a boat, so we're always out on the lake in the summer—I have a million suits. Top drawer of my dresser," she said. "Same drawer as my underwear—sorry if that's weird? I'd take you up there myself, but, like . . ." She waved a hand around, as if to say the entire party would dissolve into chaos if she went upstairs. "There's a bunch of options in there. I have too many. Pick whatever you want."

"I'm really fine," I squeaked.

"Just go," Jordan insisted. "It'll be fun. We want you to!"

"Is that for me? That's so sweet," said Bee, nodding at my gift. "Presents are on that table over there, if you want to drop it off."

"I like the festive wrapping paper," said Kaylee.

I couldn't tell if she was kidding or not. "Ho, ho, ho."

"I'll just . . ." I motioned toward the upstairs.

"Go. Come back. Be warm," Jordan said, closing her eyes.

I hurried upstairs and managed to find Bee's room without asking her parents. It had a giant BTS poster on the outside, so it wasn't that hard. Her bedroom was cute—white and purple, and hey, cool, a TV. My parents would never let me have a TV in my room in a million years. I went to her dresser and opened the top drawer, but I felt helpless, looking at yellow and pink and green bikini tops made for girls who actually needed to wear bras. I'd look ridiculous in any of these. And her underwear—God, this was weird. I'd never tell a practical stranger to go in my underwear drawer. I still had cartoon characters on some of them, for God's sake. And flowery ones that Mom would buy in a pack from Target.

And then, something hard—a frame. I pulled it out to see a photo.

Bee and Rachel and Jordan, arms thrown around each other. Rachel resting her head on Bee's shoulder. Both of them smiling at the camera.

I stared at that photo for a moment and just felt the weight of it. A photo stuffed into a drawer, but not thrown away. A frame *hidden*. This was a friendship that was missed. That much was clear.

There was a knock on the door, and I jumped about a foot in the air.

"Find anything that fits?" It was Bee. "I just came up to make sure you didn't, like, get lost or something."

I weighed my options. Should I get caught snooping in the dresser drawer of a perfectly nice girl who had invited me to her birthday party and offered to lend me a swimsuit? Or should I try to hide the photo? But there was really no way to shove it back in the drawer. It was obviously already in my hands. I racked my brain—could I just say *None of your swimsuits looked like they'd fit me, haha, I'm on my way back down*?

But just as I was about to try and play it off, her eyes landed on my hands, clutching the frame.

I held up the photo wordlessly. She stared at it, then at me, then at her feet.

"So, what, you think I'm a horrible person?" she asked. "Some kind of bully?"

"No," I said honestly. "I just wish someone would let me in on the big secret."

"There is no big secret."

"I know Rachel burned down the barn," I said. "I know that's why everyone hates her. But there has to be more to it than that, doesn't there? It was an accid—"

Bee held up her hand. "Anna, God. I'm trying to be nice to you here, okay? I've been trying since you got here. New kid and all? It's my *birthday party.* I'm trying to lend you a swimsuit. That's all. If you're gonna ask a bunch of questions . . ."

This was probably one of those moments where Mom thought I got too intense. I should back off. I should let someone have a boundary. So I just nodded, put the photo down, and grabbed a lime-green bikini that definitely wouldn't fit. It probably wouldn't even fit *Nik.*

"You need one smaller than that. No offense. Honestly, I'm jealous of you—boobs are annoying. Here." Bee walked over to her dresser and yanked out an orange-and-white-striped tankini set. It had a lot more coverage, but it was still cuter than my plain one-piece. "Try this. Then *forget* about Rachel Riley and just . . . come have fun, okay? Mimi Miller isn't here."

She disappeared back out the door. I pulled on the swimsuit, leaving my one-piece zipped up in my North Face pocket, and hurried back downstairs. Jordan scooted over when she saw me, and I slid in next to her. She was right—it did feel good.

And so I sat there, at Bee Becker's birthday party, and tried to forget that there was a girl sitting at home all alone. And when Kaylee told a story about how dumb her mom was, always forgetting things, I laughed, even though it made me feel sad. I loved my mom. I thought of her favorite fuzzy socks she'd pulled on before watching some History Channel special with my dad tonight, waving goodbye. Usually, Nik and I would both be home, the two friendless wonders, but now Nik had a whole group of nerdy coder friends, and I was here trying to be friends with Bee Becker. I wasn't the kind of person who talked crap about her family at birthday parties, even though I knew actually liking your parents wasn't that cool.

Nik had CodeHERs now. What did I have? The Rachel Riley project. An invite to Bee Becker's birthday party. And that was about it. Maybe I should have given more thought to joining Global Leaders.

It wasn't until Kaylee and Carmen were talking about some weekly game of volleyball they played with the boys at the park that I remembered what Nik had said.

"Is that *the* game?" I asked.

They all looked at me, confused.

"What game?" asked Carmen.

I shrugged. "My sister is in high school, and she

117

said some boys there had brought over some . . . game from the middle school and were playing it. I don't know if it's, like, a sport or a word game or what. But some kind of game that the boys do."

I didn't know, then, what the game was. I only knew that *knowing* suddenly settled into that hot tub like a fog—as if someone had jerked the water temperature down to freezing cold, and I had said something completely unsayable.

"I don't know what you're talking about," Kaylee said flatly. But it was the same way Bee Becker had denied being friends with Rachel Riley, way back in French class. *I don't know* can mean *I know exactly*, and right then, it did. In fact, they all had the same looks on their faces that they got whenever Rachel came up in conversation. Were they related? The game and Rachel?

Jordan quickly changed the subject to the latest Netflix movie everyone was obsessed with, and I added another tally to my screwups of eighth grade at East Middle.

"Have you seen it, Anna?" Jordan asked.

"Um . . . no. But I read the book," I said awkwardly. I hadn't liked it, actually. It was way too slow. But the other girls just blinked at me for a second before getting back to their conversation.

When it was time to open presents, I realized early I'd made another mistake. All of the presents suddenly seemed perfect—gift cards, Nike T-shirts, a pair of sweatpants with *cutie* written across the butt. When Bee opened my book, she kind of glanced at it for a second before Jordan spoke up.

"I liked that one," Jordan said. "About the whale, right? And her grandma? Not the whale's grandma . . . the girl's . . . I read it last year."

I just nodded. My cheeks felt like they were on fire. I was thankful, in that moment, for Jordan Russell and her attempted kindness. Book people—we stuck together. Jordan was always trying to make everyone feel comfortable and welcome and happy. Bee said a quick thanks and moved on to her next new pair of leggings. A book . . . It felt so weirdly personal all of a sudden. It was a completely *wrong* gift.

Why did I feel like everyone had gotten some kind of manual on being an eighth grader except for me? Why did I feel like everyone else knew exactly what kind of swimsuit to bring to birthday parties, and what kind of gift to give the birthday girl? I loved that book. I would way rather have been given it than sweatpants. I would way rather be reading it right now than surrounded by all of these other people. But I felt embarrassed for giving it, and stupid for feeling embarrassed, and for some reason, annoyed at my mom, who constantly told me to be social and make friends without reminding me that to do so I'd probably have to do things like wear a bikini and talk bad about her. Who bought me books for gifts and told me to be myself but then seemed to be kind of annoyed when I did.

All of this to say: when Nik picked me up that night, I was glad to go home. Nik was always having to drive me around. My parents would only pay her car insurance if she served as my chauffer.

"Did you have fun?" she asked.

I stared out the window. "Um . . . no. Not really."

But to my surprise, instead of a sarcastic comment or a just completely ignoring me, Nik said, "Yeah. Eighth grade sucks." Her phone buzzed, and she glanced down at it quick.

"*Texting and driving is clever, said nobody ever,*" I said in an ominous voice. It was an annoying PSA that played on TV every single commercial break.

Nik rolled her eyes. "It's not me. It's Bronson."

"The one you like?"

"I don't like him," she said, and I actually believed her. It was the way she said it: a definitive answer. "I mean . . . I like him fine, but I don't *like* him or whatever, and he texts me all the time."

"Tell him not to," I said.

"Anna," she sighed, and it was that one word—*Anna*—that meant everything little sisters hate when big sisters say. That I was dumb, and immature, and knew nothing about the real world, and brought babyish swimsuits to bikini birthday parties. So I sat the rest of the drive staring out the window, feeling bad for poor Bronson Webb and his sad, broken heart.

7

OCTOBER 18

To: Lana McLeen <lana@lanamcleen.com>
From: Principal Lila Howe <lhowe@east.middle.edu>
Subj: Winter dance!

Lana,

Howdy-ho from your princi-PAL!

Our Harvest Fest was a raging success, and due to the generosity of our fabulous Knights family, we're able to throw an eighth-grade Winter Ball this year. I know it will be absolutely DYNAMITE! Especially since their seventh-grade Spring Fling was sadly canceled. These kids deserve a rockin' good time, agreed?!

That's why when I was brainstorming chairpeople, I instantly thought of you! After all, as our resident Wedding Queen, you're sure to throw *quite* the celebration. I'm thinking we have our grand partay somewhere a bit more affordable than Kincaid Farms—in our own school gym, perhaps? I'm sure with your décor magic, you can whip it into shape! I know you're incredibly busy with your wedding season, so if you're too busy helping the blushing brides of Madison prepare for their big days, I understand. But I just know that nobody will be able to pull this off like you will!

If you agree, let's meet a week from tomorrow to discuss progress. As the chairperson, you'd be involved in the invitations, finding parent volunteers, organizing a décor committee . . . So many details to nail down!

(BTW, if you're looking for parent volunteers—that new family, the Hunts, may be a good place to start. I suggested to Maja at Harvest Fest that her participation in events would be a great way to learn the ropes of being a Knights parent, and she said that she'd be happy to, sometime in the future. Well, the future's HERE—and it's looking bright!)

Best,
Lila Howe

OCTOBER 18

To: Sierra Kincaid <skincaid@kincaidfarms.com>
From: Anna Hunt <ahunt@east.middle.edu>
Subj: Question

Ms. Kincaid,

My name is Anna Hunt and I'm an eighth-grade student at East Middle School. I'm currently doing a research project and trying to find out what exactly happened at your dairy barn last spring may be a key component of it. Would you be willing to answer a few brief questions for me about the incident?

Sincerely,
Anna Hunt

OCTOBER 19

To: LIST: Parents of East Eighth Graders

From: Principal Lila Howe <lhowe@east.middle.edu>

Subj: Today's vandalism

Parents of East Middle School Eighth Graders,

It saddens my heart deeply to have to reach out and ask for your assistance to keep East Middle School a peaceful, pleasant place for learning. I'm sure that many of your children have already informed you about the vandalism found on a student's locker this morning. Destroying school property and bullying are both completely unacceptable. Although we haven't found the culprit, rest assured that we are doing everything we can to locate him/her and bring this matter to justice.

If any of your children are feeling uncomfortable about today's events, please remind them that Dr. Fayen, our guidance counselor, is always available to chat.

Best,
Lila Howe

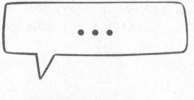

OCTOBER 19

Cody:
Did u write that stupid
message on the locker??
RACHEL RILEY IS A FREAK?
That's not even creative

Blake:
Lol definitely not. Are you kidding
me?????? If I got busted for that my
dad would kill me

Cody:
Well then who did?

Blake:
Idk man! Why are you always
freaking out about her? You do
realize she totally ruined our
spring dance? Plus she threatened
to get me SUSPENDED. AND you.
Don't forget that

Cody:
I haven't forgotten. Trust me.
I think about it every day.
Just leave her alone

Blake:
Whatever u say, Romeo

OCTOBER 19

To: Sierra Kincaid <skincaid@kincaidfarms.com>

From: Anna Hunt <ahunt@east.middle.edu>

Subj: Fwd: Question

Hi Ms. Kincaid,

I just wanted to check in and see if you saw my last email. I could really use your help!

Sincerely,

Anna Hunt

"NIK!"

I banged on her bedroom door as hard as I could, but no answer. That meant she was in Serious Coder Mode: door locked, noise-canceling earbuds in. Back in Chicago, I could have easily jiggled the lock with a knife, but our new doors didn't do that.

I went around to our backyard to get her attention through the window. It was *cold*, too—late October meant that winter was right around the corner, just starting to tap us on the shoulder. I crunched through the leaves to the backyard, pulling my sweatshirt sleeves down over my hands, and stuck my face in her window.

Nik wasn't even coding. She was just lying on her bed, staring up at the ceiling, with her earbuds in.

I waved through the window and finally caught her eye. She gave me a *what on earth are you doing out there* look, and I gave her a frustrated *you didn't open the door* look right back.

She walked over to the window and yanked it open.

"Oh my God, *what*?" she said. "What's the *emergency*? What's *so* important?"

I glared at her. "You're not even doing anything. Just lying down on your bed."

"Yeah, and lesson learned: next time I need to close the curtains. I was *thinking*, if you must know. Now what do you want?"

"A ride," I said.

"Ask Mom."

"I did. She's having some other mom over from school to talk about the Winter Ball." When Mom told me she was helping organize the dance, I was pretty sure she had hidden a secret camera somewhere to record my reaction for a viral YouTube video. Mom just . . . wasn't one of those moms. I *loved* my mom— loved the way she listened, and the way she cared about people so deeply, and the way she worked harder than anyone I'd ever met—but she wasn't exactly the classroom mom, you know? *I work*, she reminded me endlessly when I asked her about volunteering for field trips or class parties. So eventually, I'd just kind of stopped asking.

"She's *what*?" asked Nik.

"Don't ask," I said. "She said Principal Howe ambushed her at Harvest Fest, and Lana McLeen promised her it wouldn't be that much work."

"Lana McLeen, Wedding Queen?" asked Nik, wrinkling her nose.

"Exactly. The billboard." The truth was, I wasn't even sure I wanted to go to the dance. But now that Mom was volunteering, I felt like I had to. If I'd felt out of place at Bee's birthday party, how was I going to feel at a place that was specifically designed for teenage hormones and adolescent anxiety? I mean, how many horror movies had scenes that took place at dances? It was an event primed for embarrassment.

Nik rolled her eyes. "I'm busy."

"You are not!"

"Well, where do you need to go?"

"The library," I said.

"Go next weekend. You have a million books."

"I can't. It's for a school project."

Nik just stared at me, and here's the thing—I should have known. Obviously, my grand plan wasn't going to work.

Because I didn't *really* have to go to the library. But the library was only one bus stop away from

Kincaid Farms. And I *had* to go back there and ask someone about the fire. My emails had gone completely unanswered.

But say what you will about sisters—they know you.

"Why in the world would you need to go to a public library for a school project?" she asked.

"Primary sources," I said.

She narrowed her eyes. "Um, hello? It's called the internet archives. What kind of project is it?"

"It's on . . ." I glanced around the backyard. A goose family was waddling by—a mom, with four or five of her little goose babies. Good thing Kix wasn't outside. They would have been dead meat. It reminded me of my science project.

"Penguins," I said. "My penguin thing."

Nik laughed. "Yeah, okay. How about this? Tell me where you *really* need to be, and I'll *consider* driving you."

"That is where I need to be!"

She reached forward to pull the window back down.

"Wait! Okay, okay." I ran my hands up and down my arms, trying to stay warm. "I need to go to Kincaid Farms. It's for my Rachel Riley project, okay? I just didn't know if . . . if Mom would like it. I think she thinks I'm being too intense." In fact—I *knew* she thought I was being too intense.

"I thought you weren't even allowed to do that project," Nik said.

"It's not for school. It's on my own."

"You're invading some girl's privacy and running around like Nancy Drew just for kicks?"

Could I tell my sister about the podcasting summit? On one hand, she'd probably be helpful. Like now, when I needed a ride, or later, when I'd definitely need help on the tech end of things. But on the other hand, she'd sold me out to Mom for heinous crimes such as forgetting to take the dogs out or finishing the last of the milk. Who knew what she'd do with information I actually found *important*?

"It's complicated," I said.

Nik stared at me, and for a second, I thought she was going to slam the window back closed.

Instead, she told me to get my coat.

It was a Saturday, which meant there was a wedding. Duh—I should have thought of that. The parking lot was overflowing with cars, and I could see a huge chalkboard sign welcoming us to the Cisneros/ Carmichael wedding.

"Hashtag TomasGetsMaryd," read Nik. "Um . . . yikes." On the drive over, I'd told her about Mimi Miller. She loved *Story of Our Lives*, too. She still seemed hesitant about my investigation. But she did say it would be cool to get to participate in the podcasting summit in Chicago.

"We have to find Sierra Kincaid," I said as she pulled up behind a minivan and parked. "She's the person who runs the events barn."

"We can't just go running around a wedding in jeans and North Faces," hissed Nik.

"Then stay in the car," I told her, hopping out. "I'll be quick."

But she got out with me, and we traipsed across the dirt-paved parking lot. The barn really was beautiful—it looked completely different than it had for Harvest Fest. Gone were the giant hay barrels and carnival games—instead there was a huge white table covered with silver-wrapped presents, a sparkly photo booth, and a long buffet table.

"Um, can I help you?" A woman wearing a headset glanced over at us. She was holding a clipboard.

"We're . . . I'm looking for Sierra Kincaid," I said.

"Sierra? She's on-site somewhere, but I couldn't tell you where. This is a private event, anyway. You'll have to call her next week."

"But—"

"*Hannah!*" A woman with dreadlocks in a long emerald colored gown ran up to us. "Level-seven emergency. Her bustle broke, and—"

"I have plenty of safety pins. I'm on my way," the woman said calmly. She turned back to us. "Sorry, but if you're not a guest of the Cisneros or Carmichael families, I'm going to have to ask you to—"

"Thanks anyway!" I said quickly, grabbing my sister's elbow and yanking her away. It was like we were spies on a secret mission, like when Tris snuck into Erudite headquarters in *Divergent*.

"She told us to leave," hissed Nik, as we made our way farther into the crowd.

"No. She was *about* to tell us to leave. And anyway, I see her." Sierra was standing behind the bar, talking pointedly to three guys with beards.

"How do you know that's her?"

"LinkedIn creeping. Come on." I hurried to the bar, Nik trying to keep up behind me.

"Excuse me. Ms. Kincaid?" I said, knocking on the bar.

She glanced our way. "The bar isn't open until after the ceremony. Apologies. Also, soda and water will actually be over on the other end of the barn, unless you use some miracle age-defying cream I need to learn more about."

"Actually, I'm . . ." I'm . . . what? Doing a project on the arsonist who burned down your place of work? A thirteen-year-old who saw you at Harvest Fest for five seconds? A concerned citizen who wanted to end bullying in its multitude of forms?

"I'm a friend of Rachel Riley's" is what came out of my mouth.

She froze. Her eyes narrowed slightly.

"You're the girl who's been emailing me, aren't you? I'm very busy, as you can see," she said, motioning with her hand. "We have a major event today. So . . . stay away from the matches and kindly see yourself out."

"I was just—I was wondering . . . if I could talk to you? About what happened. I did a ton of googling, but I couldn't really figure out if you ever learned why she did it."

"I thought you said you were her friend," she snapped. "So ask her. But no, I didn't learn why, and guess what? I don't care. Insurance more than paid for the damage, I didn't press charges for trespassing out of the goodness of my heart, and I'm trying to run a business here. What that girl did made my entire summer a nightmare. Have you ever overseen a rush construction job of a barn because you had

137

an entire event schedule booked for September and October? *With* three older brothers who happen to be extremely opinionated, and an entire dairy operation to run?"

"Um." I wasn't sure if I was supposed to answer. "No."

She pointed a finger at me. "No, you haven't. And with all due respect, the last thing I need on my property is another middle schooler with an agenda. So please see yourself out." She turned away from me completely, 180 degrees, and got back to the bearded bartenders. One of them winced in my direction as if to say, *Sorry, kid.*

But I had gotten the answer to my question.

Sierra Kincaid had no idea why Rachel Riley had burned down the barn, either.

"What I don't get," said Nik, driving us back home, "is what she was doing there in the first place. Even if it *was* an accident . . . why was she trespassing in a barn, by herself, in the middle of the night?"

"I don't know," I admitted. "I mean, people do stupid things, right? Things that don't make sense."

"With friends? Sure," said Nik. "I mean, kids do dumb stuff in groups all the time. But by yourself?"

"And the place—it's too much of a coincidence. The night before a big dance?" I stared out the window. "It's not adding up."

"It feels like she had a plan," said Nik. "I know she said it was an accident, but being at the barn, by yourself, the night before some huge event . . ."

"You're right."

"Anyway, these kids seem kind of mean sometimes, from what you've told me," she said. "A sabotage thing, maybe?" She honked her horn at the Corvette in front of us, where the driver was happily texting on her phone instead of paying attention to stop signs. Her license plate read *FITN3SS*. What does it say about you that you love "fitn3ss" so much you put it on your license plate?

"Maybe Rachel Riley had her reasons," I said.

"Maybe Rachel Riley had *good* reasons. Middle schoolers aren't exactly the greatest people to be around. She could have been sending someone a message," Nik replied.

Her phone buzzed for the eight millionth time since we'd left. She didn't even glance at it.

"Is that your Romeo?" I asked.

"*Bronson.* Why do we use Romeo as an example, anyway? We're reading that in English right now.

He falls in love with Juliet in about three seconds because he thinks she's hot. Not exactly romantic."

"I saw the movie. The Leonardo DiCaprio version. Speaking of annoying guys, I thought you were going to tell him to stop texting you."

"I never said that. *You* said that. Anyway," she said, as she turned Mom's Camry into the driveway, "you should have brought home a book or something. For your 'project,'" she said.

"Internet archives," I said with a grin. "Turns out I didn't need the library after all."

There was a shiny silver Subaru parked where Mom's car usually went, and when we got inside, there she was—Lana McLeen, Wedding Queen, sipping coffee at our kitchen table.

"Girls," said Mom, nodding. "You find what you need?"

"Sort of," I said.

"These are my daughters, Nikola and Anna," Mom told Lana. "Anna's the eighth grader, obviously."

"Hello, girls," said Lana. "Nice to meet you. Anna, you must know my son, Cody."

"Not well," I admitted. "But we've . . . met."

"I was just telling your mom about that dreadful graffiti on Tuesday," Lana said.

I winced, remembering it. Bright red letters.

Rachel Riley's a freak. Scrawled across her locker, but big enough that it covered about six. Her face, just seeing it, not even reacting. She was tough, Rachel Riley. You had to give her that.

"Yeah. I felt really bad," I said. "I hope they catch who did it."

"Cody was so upset," said Lana. "But he insisted he knew nothing about it. It's all so hard on him," she said in an almost-whisper to my mom. "They were such good friends for so long."

"Cody and Rachel?" I asked.

Lana glanced at me, surprised, and I could see my mom's tired face. *Cool it, Anna.*

"The Rileys are our next-door neighbors," said Lana. "Cody and Rachel were inseparable for years. The best of friends. I mean, vacations together, the whole nine yards. But, you know . . ." She waved her hands. "Kids fall out, especially girls and boys. She got very serious about her violin, and Cody's more of an athlete. And that nasty business with the fire." She shuddered. "The Rileys are a nice family, though. When Greg had his heart attack last year, Kristy brought us groceries for weeks. Good eggs."

That nasty business with the fire.

"So . . ." I started, but my mom held up a hand.

"That's enough, Anna," she said. "Lana and I are

working. Here's what we *really* need your help with: a silver-and-blue color scheme, or a purple-and-gold one?" Lana bent her head to type something into her phone, and Mom gagged at me, a *Can you believe I have to do this?* look. But I just turned around and left, going up to my room, Lana's words about Cody and Rachel banging around in my head.

8

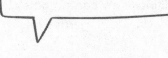

OCTOBER 23

Anna:
Do you have Kaylee's number??

Bee:
Yup! Here

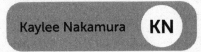

Kaylee Nakamura   KN

Anna:
Thanks I think her dog is in our backyard. I recognize him from her Instagram stories.

Bee:
OMG!!! Call her! She's been SO upset.
I've felt really bad for her!

Anna:
I let our dogs out and they
wouldn't stop barking, and
then I saw this other dog just
chilling in my dad's veggie
garden lol.

OCTOBER 23

Anna: This is WHAT HAPPENED TO RACHEL RILEY?: AN INVESTIGATION BY ANNA HUNT.
Please introduce yourself to our listeners.

Kaylee: Is this going to be public?

Anna: No.

Kaylee: Then . . . who are your listeners?

Anna: I'm . . . not sure. The judges, I guess. Anyway. Can you explain why you're talking to me?

Kaylee: I just . . . I mean, I feel bad. I don't think I've been the nicest to you this year. And then you found my dog, and I—you have no idea what Kolbe means to me. He's sort of, like, my best friend, even though I know that sounds dumb. He's a dog. But dogs can be really good listeners, you know? And dogs don't care what you wear, or what grades you get, or how funny you are. They just like you for no reason at all. And it was my fault he got out, because I know he can't help himself around squirrels, and I still let him off his leash for a minute. I just thought he needed the freedom. But then he took off, and I was terrified I was never going to see my best friend again. And then you called me. When my stepmom and I pulled up—I mean, you saw me! I was bawling.

Anna: You were happy. I get it. I love my dogs, too.

Kaylee: Yeah. But then I just felt really, really bad about not being that welcoming to you. It's not that I don't like you. I don't even know you. So . . . I mean, thanks for finding my dog. But also—I don't know. I don't know! Maybe we should talk about this stuff. Maybe we should tell somebody else what happened last spring. It's just that it was so hard on a lot of us and we're not really over it. And we don't really want to explain it to the new kid, you know? We just kind of want to be over it. But it's not really over with, it feels like, because even though it stopped, nobody ever got in any trouble. And I'm not saying they should have. But . . . it's kind of like Ms. O'Dell said in Social Issues. History is just people making mistakes and then sometimes trying to fix them, over and over and over.

Anna: That's my favorite class.

Kaylee: Mine too. My dad says it's a waste of taxpayer dollars, but I look forward to it every single day. I like that we can say whatever we're thinking and have conversations about stuff we actually care about. I don't always feel like I can do that at, you know, lunch or whatever. That class makes me feel like—I don't know. Like we have a part to play in the world. Even though we're thirteen.

Anna: So you feel like you needed to help fix a mistake?

Kaylee: Most days I still want to just . . . not talk about it. But you're like a real podcaster. You keep asking questions! And sometimes I just want to chill out and be at a birthday party, you know?

Anna: I didn't bring up Rachel at the birthday party!

Kaylee: First of all, Bee totally told me you did upstairs. And you brought up the game. Same difference. And I've been thinking about it ever since.

Anna: The game? Oh, wait, yeah—the game. Did that have to do with Rachel?

Kaylee: Yeah. I was kind of mad at you for bringing it up. But that wasn't fair. You didn't know. You don't know.

Anna: Don't know what?

Kaylee: What the game is . . . and what it has to do with Rachel Riley.

Anna: And that's what you're here to tell me?

Kaylee: Right. But only as a thank-you for finding

Kolbe, okay? You can't tell anybody I told you. It's— We don't like to talk about it. Our whole class. So you can't share this with anyone at school.

Anna: I won't.

Kaylee: Swear. Swear on your dogs. Nobody but the Northwestern people.

Anna: I swear on my dogs.

Kaylee: <deep breath> *Okay. Sorry. I'm a little nervous.*

Anna: Take your time.

Kaylee: Around winter break of last year . . . a few of the boys started doing this weird thing. Not all of them, but some of them. Mainly that one group—Blake and Riz and their friends? Carlos, Trevor . . .

Anna: Right. That group.

Kaylee: They'd do this weird thing, and they'd keep track of who did it the most.

Anna: What was the weird thing?

Kaylee: It was—this sounds so stupid. Oh my God. Whatever. It was slapping people on the butt.

Anna: It was . . . what?

Kaylee: Slapping people on the butt! Girls. Slapping girls on the butt. And different girls were worth different points.

Anna: What do you mean?

Kaylee: Like, the prettier the girl was, the more

points she was worth. So, Jordan, Rachel, me—no offense, I didn't make the game—we got high points. Jordan and Rachel especially. They really had it out for those two. But someone like . . . I don't know, I don't want to be mean. Other people weren't worth as many points.

Anna: Okay . . . like, when would they do this?

Kaylee: Whenever. Hallways. Lunch.

Anna: At school?

Kaylee: Mostly. But if they saw you outside of school at a football game or whatever, that counted, too.

Anna: I bet you guys got really mad.

Kaylee: I mean, it was weird. But it was a joke, you know? They're our friends. It was funny. <silence> Actually, I mean, it wasn't that funny. I don't know why I said that. I guess that's just . . . what you say when something makes you feel weird. That it was funny.

Anna: I get that. I do that, too.

Kaylee: Everyone does, I think. Every girl does. Or maybe not every girl, but I did. I laughed about it. Haha, they're dumb, cavemen, grow a brain . . . you know, whatever. Jordan and I, we aren't those girls that get upset over every little thing. It's just who the boys are. That group of boys, anyway.

Anna: How did they keep track of points?

Kaylee: This is—this part is weird, okay? I mean,

if someone heard this, something really bad could happen. Like, they could get in big trouble. That's why you can't tell a soul. I should have had you sign one of those forms, so if you tell anyone at school I can sue you for a million dollars.

Anna: Good try, but I don't have a million dollars.

Kaylee: Ha. So, they had a website. With the points. And, like, a running tally. You know, Riz has fifteen points this week, but oops, next week Blake has twenty-five, so he's winning.

Anna: Why is them having a website such a big deal? I mean, I get that then someone could find it and they'd get in trouble, but is it a bigger deal than actually doing the slapping?

Kaylee: Because cyberbullying? Hello? All the assemblies, the posters, the documentaries? Don't your parents shove that stuff down your throat?

Anna: Um, not exactly.

Kaylee: Well, mine do. So I know that once you take something like this and put it online . . . it's bad news. Some kids in Ohio once went to jail for creating a website about this kid they didn't like.

Anna: What did you win if you got the most points?

Kaylee: Nothing. Well—nothing.

Anna: What?

Kaylee: I said nothing. The points were dumb.

They'd get . . . I don't know. Fame and glory.

Anna: Okay, but what does any of this have to do with Rachel?

Kaylee: I don't know for sure. But a lot of people think that's why she burned down the barn. Because she wanted to punish the boys by canceling the dance. She cared about the game—she hated it more than anybody else. And then the day after the fire . . . Blake had a note in his locker, telling him if he didn't stop the game right away, someone was going to show the website to Principal Howe. So everyone kind of thought it was her.

Anna: But there's no proof that that's why she did it.

Kaylee: No, but there's no proof she didn't, either. And she never denied it. All she had to do was say, Haha, here's why I was in the barn, this is all a big misunderstanding! *But she never did. So obviously, it's true.*

Anna: But . . . I get why that would make Blake mad at her. Why would everyone else be?

Kaylee: It was our dance, too.

Anna: Right. But it was just a dance.

Kaylee: First of all, Anna, it wasn't just a dance. It was the seventh-grade Spring Fling, which is when they hand out all of the class awards, and it's basically the best night of the entire year and something you look forward to seventh grade for. But also . . . it wasn't only that. It was that she took something that was just a joke and made it this huge thing. Something worth burning down a barn over. Something worth threatening Blake over. She took it all so seriously. And I guess—I don't know. It made a part of me feel bad for not taking it seriously. And that made me mad. I'm not really making any sense, am I?

Anna: Wow. Okay. Sorry, I'm just . . . taking a lot in.

Kaylee: You see why we don't like to talk about it? It feels good, though. Telling you. It feels really, really good.

I WENT ON A WALK AFTER I TALKED TO KAYLEE. A LONG
one, around our neighborhood. I didn't even know where
I was going. Kaylee lived only a few streets away, but
instead of going right home, I found myself wandering,
up and down streets, looking at the pretty, ginormous
houses on the shore of Lake Mendota. Houses painted
different colors, with political signs in the front yards
and wind chimes on the porches. I had to move my
legs, which would maybe move my brain. Walks, show-
ers, long car rides, they *do* something to you, to help
you think. And I couldn't stop thinking.

My phone started buzzing. It was almost time for
dinner. I was later than I'd said I'd be. People would
be getting worried—Mom, Dad, maybe even Nik. People who loved me. People who wanted me to be safe,
safe from fires and butt slaps.

But you're *not* safe, once you leave your house,
are you? Unless you're one of those people whose parents kept you in a big old hamster bubble, constantly
handing you hand sanitizer and not letting you drink

from water fountains. There were cars that could hit you and lightning that could strike you. There were sandboxes with sharp edges. We were supposed to be scared of Blake Wyatt and his friends, too? Blake, who had Iron Man stickers on his binder? Who was more dangerous—him with his hands or Rachel Riley with a lighter? Which one of them wasn't allowed to go to Harvest Fest?

You can't really feel safe in this world, is what I was learning. Protection is flimsy. The people who are supposed to shield you from danger might not. A flame of anger can become a fire and burn down an entire barn.

Help me, Babcia, I thought. Because at that moment, I missed her so badly. My *babcia*, with her giant knitted afghans and little house slippers. She'd make me apple pancakes and real tea, with caffeine, and we'd sit and talk.

I kind of felt like Babcia would slap Blake Wyatt across the face if he touched her butt. You should hear her talk about the communists who ran Poland when she was growing up—she could get angry, for an old lady, her hands waving around and her face all red. But then, aren't we supposed to forgive? Treat others as they would unto you, etc.? Turn the other cheek?

Babcia may have slapped Blake Wyatt, but she also had a crucifix above every door in her house. Rosaries, too; entire drawers of them.

The buzz from my phone brought my thoughts back to America. Six missed calls. I finally pulled it out of my pocket and answered it, sitting on a rock in some random person's front yard.

"Hi, Dad," I said.

"Anna Maria Hunt, where are you? The roast is going to be ready in five minutes. You were supposed to come home right after you talked to your friend. It's been hours!"

"I know. I'm sorry."

"It's getting *dark*."

"I know! I went on a walk. I wasn't thinking."

"Well . . . where are you? Can you walk home? Geez, you freaked me out. I've been listening to too many podcasts. Your mom has me hooked on one about this doctor who kills people during surgery."

"I'm not in surgery. I'm over by the lake. I can walk home."

"Not when it's getting this dark. I'll send your sister to pick you up."

"No! I'll pretend to talk on the phone the whole way," I said. "Bad guys won't get you when you're on the phone." I'm not sure why I said that, but Dad must have bought it, because I found myself hurrying home, pressing my phone to my ear.

And as I walked, I wondered if Blake Wyatt had to think about that as *he* walked home. If *he* had to press his phone to his ear in the dark so no bad guys would get him.

9

NOVEMBER 1

To: Katarzyna Kowalski <babciakat@gmail.com>
From: Anna Hunt <ahunt@east.middle.edu>
Subj: Things I like

Babcia,

I liked your list. It reminded me of all the reasons I miss you, too. You said a reason you miss me is because I was fearless, but I'm not feeling so fearless these days, to tell you the truth. I'm kind of feeling like Jesse at a new dog park. Remember when you visited us in Chicago two years ago and we took him to that one that had that big old angry dog? It kept looking at

Jesse like he was about to pounce. He just hid behind our legs the whole time. He wouldn't even go get his tennis ball when I threw it.

Yesterday was Halloween, and Bee asked if I wanted to come over and watch scary movies with her and some of her friends. But I just stayed in and watched a documentary on the Salem witch trials with Mom and Dad. We kept getting interrupted by trick-or-treaters, so honestly, I can't really tell you much about Salem, except that a really long time ago a bunch of rich teenage girls accused poor people of being witches and got them burned at the stake. It's messed up.

Okay, my turn.

Things I Miss About Chicago:

My old school. It wasn't like I had tons of friends or anything, but at least I felt comfortable there. Meeting people over and over again is just so tiring. I should get the words *Yeah, we moved here from Chicago. Yup, it's a lot different* tattooed on my arm so I can stop saying them.

The lake. They have lakes here, too, duh. We have two big lakes in Madison, and they're even pretty. But if I want to see Lake Michigan, we have to drive all the way to Milwaukee. I always felt like we lived by the ocean. I like looking out at a body of water so big you can't put your arms around it.

All of the Polish people constantly speaking Polish. It's English, English, English all the time. The other day I forgot the word for "lamp." I had to describe it to Nik—*that thing with the light.*

City life. Madison's fine, but it doesn't have Michigan Avenue. The *noise*, too. I can't sleep at night here. It's too quiet. I've been up so late every single night, I even asked Dad if I could have coffee the other morning. He said no, but I bought a soda as soon as I got to school.

Myself, kind of. Just waking up and knowing exactly who I am and exactly where I belong. Does that sound weird? I wake up here and just feel all itchy, like I'm waiting for something.

I hope any of this makes any sense. I miss, miss, miss you, more than I miss Chicago. Way more.

Good guesses on the penguin researcher. But Jane Goodall does monkeys, not penguins. I was referring to Edward Wilson. He was one of the first people to witness the breeding practices of emperor penguins, all the way back in 1901. He walked through Antarctica in negative-seventy-six-degree weather in 1911 to retrieve some penguin eggs that he could bring back to London. Those poor little eggs—lifted from their nests and taken to an entirely new place. They didn't even survive the journey. Edward Wilson was kind of a jerk. He took out the embryos and gave them to the Natural History Museum in London. They weren't able to be born, and they couldn't just keep being eggs, either, since Edward Wilson had taken them out. They were frozen in time in London for years.

Love,
Anna

NOVEMBER 1

Kaylee:
I have to tell you something and I feel like you're gonna be mad.

Jordan:
??

Kaylee:
I told Anna about the game.

Kaylee:
Please don't be mad. I'M SORRY. She found Kolbe and I just felt like I owed her big. She was actually really nice about it and it felt good to tell someone.

Jordan:
. . . ok . . .

Jordan:
You should have told me
last night at Bee's.

Kaylee:
It might go in her project bc I did like an
interview thing on her phone. PLEASE
DON'T BE MAD!!! It's for some summer
camp thing. It doesn't even have to do
with school. Anna said she won't tell
anyone

Kaylee:
Jordan??

Kaylee:
I'm sorry!!!!!

I STARED AT THE SHEET OF PAPER IN MY HANDS. Looked up the hallways, too: left, right, left again, like I was crossing the street. But there was nobody there. Just Eleanor, our ancient janitor, who looked too old to go grocery shopping alone, let alone mop up barf and empty the garbage cans.

Lunch had ended. I had sat at my usual spot, on the other end of Rachel Riley's lunch table. She nodded to me, and I nodded back, and she pulled out a book and started reading.

But when it was time to go outside, I just didn't feel like standing around by myself. I figured I'd get my math notebook and go get some homework done in the library. When I opened my locker, a piece of paper had fluttered to the ground. It had been torn out of someone's notebook and written with a scrawl. There it was: a website.

The website. Probably.

Someone wanted me to see it. Kaylee? No, she would have just told me when we talked, right?

163

Someone else was trying to help.

I pulled out my phone, but Eleanor loudly cleared her throat. I put my phone back in my pocket—the last thing I needed right now was for it to wind up in Principal Howe's office. I'd have to look at home.

The rest of the day, that piece of paper felt hot in my pocket, like it was going to burn a hole there. I kept looking at other kids' papers, trying to see their handwriting. Was the person who gave it to me trying to tell on someone? I considered cutting class and going to the library to use a computer there, but what if they somehow tracked it back to me? I mean, you couldn't so much as go on TikTok on a school computer. They blocked *everything*.

I hurried home from school as fast as I could. Sometimes, I'd take the long way—go past the cool houses on Atwood, maybe even stop and grab a muffin from Daisy Cafe. Walking home was one of the things I actually liked best about living in Madison— in Chicago, I'd always had to take the bus. But today I was practically sprinting. The leaves had all been raked, and now things were just cold and gray. Halloween was over, and all of the jack-o'-lantern stickers in store windows had been replaced with turkeys.

When I got home, I hurried upstairs and pulled out my laptop. I typed in the URL, and—

Nothing.

The page was completely empty.

Just a big, white sheet of emptiness.

I tried clicking my mouse a few times. Refreshing. Used Chrome instead of Safari. Nada. Zilch.

I knew whose help I needed. But she wouldn't be home from CodeHERs for hours.

Nik was Miss Popular now, like I'd told Babcia—Mom and Dad were thrilled. We'd been eating more and more dinners just the three of us, and I couldn't believe how much I found myself missing my crabby older sister. Finally, she got dropped off by someone's red minivan, laughing as she hopped out. The girl who was driving honked right as Nik rounded the bumper, making her jump. She ran inside, and I practically tackled her.

"I need your help," I said. "Now. Like, right now."

"Oh my God, relax. I'm starving," she said. "What did you guys eat? Is there any left?"

"Turkey chili in the fridge," Mom said, without looking up from the papers she was grading. "Daddy added Tabasco to his, if you want to walk on the wild side."

"Yum. Where *is* Dad?"

"He took Kix to the dog park to get some energy out," said Mom. Jesse was curled up by her feet, looking pleased that his nemesis was nowhere to be seen.

"It can't wait, Nik," I said. "It's for school."

"Tell me it's not algebra," said my sister, opening the fridge and taking out a Tupperware of chili. "I can't ever solve for x."

"It's a computer thing," I said. *"Please . . ."*

"Okay, okay. Let me eat. Then I'm all ears."

I sat on the couch next to Mom and tried to read the latest Laurie Morrison book, but I kept watching Nik shovel chili in her mouth. When she finally stuck her bowl in the dishwasher, I slammed my book shut.

"Fine," she said. "My room. You can tell me where the fire is." Fire. Ha. If she only knew.

Nik's room was still comforting to me, even though it kind of felt like the command deck of a spaceship. All of those screens blinking at you, and her giant poster of Captain Moonbeard from *Planet Pirates*.

"I need you to help me find a website," I told her. "I keep trying to bring it up and it's not working."

"Okay. What's the URL?"

I told her. "Thescorecard.com."

"What's it a scorecard for?"

"Um. Just—a game."

Nik stopped.

"That's going to need a little more explanation, Anna. You're not exactly a gamer."

"Maybe I've got a new hobby."

"Maybe I wasn't born yesterday, and this has something to do with your Rachel Riley obsession."

I hadn't meant to tell Nik the whole entire story, but I did. It came pouring out—Rachel, and Kaylee's story, and Blake Wyatt. Finding Kolbe. The game— the game she had heard about, and what it was. Her face went pale, like she was going to throw up.

"This is serious stuff," said Nik. "Anna! This isn't—like, this isn't a *joke*. This is *harassment*."

"Harassment?" That word sounded too big and ugly for this situation. Harassment brought up pictures of guys in parking garages, wearing backward baseball caps. Beefy construction workers or stalkers who call you ninety-seven thousand times a day. Not Blake Wyatt and Riz Kapoor. Harassment was something people went to jail and wound up on the news for, not something that happened every single day at every middle school on the planet.

"Um, *yeah*," she said. "Did the girls tell them to stop?"

"It doesn't sound like it. Not really," I said.

Nik shook her head. "Man, I can't believe those

girls were already having to deal with that. You still have *recess*."

"It's called 'outdoor time,'" I snapped back.

"Anna. Did you tell anyone about this?"

"No! Who was I supposed to tell? What was I supposed to say? That kind of stuff—it happens all the time." It did. A million and one times. Comments on butts, jokes about bra straps. Chelsea Garcia's lavender-colored underwear peeking over the back of her jeans as she bent over to pick up a dropped pencil, and Blake calling her *purple people eater* for weeks. These things were just folded into our everyday lives, part of walking and breathing and doing math homework and eating lunch. Boys taking, and girls laughing. Having to pretend to be on your phone as you walked home in the dark.

"You have to tell someone about this," said Nik.

"Oh my God. Like *who*? Principal *Howe*?" I couldn't even picture walking into her office covered in posters of fluffy white kittens reminding me that a journey begins with a single step. Opening my mouth, telling her about what had truly gone down last year. Telling her about Blake and Riz and Trevor, doing what they wanted, taking what they saw. Watching her round up the boys and walk them down to her office. *Suspension*, maybe.

"I don't know," she said, throwing her hands up. "Or, like, a counselor? Hey—Mom. Mom would know what to do."

Mom *did* always know what to do. But Mom also was stressed, so tired coming home from campus every day with piles of ungraded essays. Mom wanted me to be making friends, not obsessing over boys grabbing girls' butts, right?

I shook my head. "If—I mean, it didn't happen to *me*."

Nik looked at me, exasperated. I was exasperated with myself. I heard it, my own voice, saying things I didn't believe. Like we could all just not care about things that didn't happen to *us*? But Sabrina, back in science class, giving me the cold shoulder because of the whole Special K thing. Mom's happy face when I told her I got invited to Bee Becker's birthday party. This wasn't like a French quiz, where there was a right or wrong answer. There were consequences to different choices, a hurricane of pros and cons. People who would be proud and people who would be disappointed.

"I'm not kidding around, Anna. This is real. This is scary crap, okay? We have to do *something*."

"It's over," I said. "It is! I haven't seen it happen this year. Other stuff, yeah, but no . . . butt slaps. Not a single one."

Nik stared at me, and I stared back.

"Are you lying to me?" she asked.

"No."

"Anna."

"I'm not!"

She sighed. "I still think you need to tell someone. But okay. I'll help you find this website. Maybe we can even find out who made it."

"There's a way to do that?" I asked, surprised.

"Oh yeah. A thousand ways," she said.

Nik always surprised me with tech stuff. The internet seemed like the Wild West to me, this infinite space where anything could happen and people went rogue. My sister always seemed to see it more clearly.

"So, first things first. If you're going to a random website some stranger put in your locker—you shouldn't look *alone*. Especially you, who, no offense, has no idea what she's doing. Anyone in the world could have given you that website, and the internet . . . it's full of strange stuff. Creeps—I mean, they're everywhere. People throw up anything they want to on the web. You have to proceed with caution."

She clicked a couple of keys on her laptop and I nodded along.

"All right. Let's see what we're working with." She brought up the site, and it was the same as what I got—blank. She did all my tricks, too, switching browsers and restarting things. She narrowed her eyes.

"I told you," I groaned.

"Oh, please. Have a little *faith*, sister mine. We just need to go wayback."

"What?"

"Wayback? The Wayback Machine. It's an internet archive." She pulled up a new website and typed the URL I had been given into a search box. A calendar appeared with some highlighted days. She clicked on one, and there it was—

The scorecard. A picture of it, anyway.

It was a pretty basic, simple site. It was just black-and-white, almost like a Word document. Down the left was a list of names I recognized: Blake, Carlos, Trevor, Riz. Others, too. Then, a number next to each name. Blake was winning, which made me shudder.

"This is the last day the Wayback Machine combed through it," she said. "Back in . . . early May. So good news for us: whatever dummy made the site didn't actually delete it. They just scrubbed it. Took off everything that was on it, but they still own the domain. Whoever bought 'thescorecard.com' had to put in a credit card number at some point. We need to see who it's registered to."

My sister was a wizard. With a few more clicks, she told me the person had paid for private registration, meaning we couldn't access their name.

"You can pay extra to keep things private," she explained. "So we can't see who paid for it."

"Now we're *really* stuck," I guessed.

Nik glanced at me. "What do I tell you about teenagers with a laptop and enough time on their hands?"

"That they could bring down the entire global economy."

"Exactly. So patience, padawan," she said. "We can still view the source of the website. I just have to open Developer Tools in Chrome . . ." *Click-clickity-click*. Her hands flew across her keyboard. "Look—we can just view the page source and see who the author is." A whole page of numbers and letters came up that looked like total gobbledygook to me.

"How are you *doing* this?" I asked her.

"A website is just a file," Nik explained to me. "Layers of code, you know? And like I said, whoever made this one isn't exactly a professional. It's not like it's hard to make a website. They teach you how in

Computer Literacy in high school. The CodeHERs girls could make a more sophisticated site than this, and they're just learning. There're plenty of ways to try and hide your identity. But look, right here: it says who the author is."

I looked over her shoulder to the text she'd highlighted. "It just says BilboBaggins1201."

Nik laughed. "Bilbo, like from *Lord of the Rings*? The short guy—what are those called again? Hoboes?"

"Hobbits. Read your Tolkien like a proper nerd."

"You know I'm more of a Marvel girl. Anyway, that's this person's coder tag. Their signature. Like, mine isn't Nikola Hunt, it's NikKnax. It's kind of like when authors use a pen name."

"Why?"

"It can just be a way of staying anonymous, if someone wants."

"So, it *doesn't* tell us who the author is."

"Now, finding out who that tag belongs to is a little trickier," she admitted. "I can see from the IP address that it's someone in Madison, which is obvious. It's got to be one of the kids at your school. But I'd have to do a lot more digging to try and find their other stuff on the web and figure out who they are. I need some time."

I groaned. "How much time? Because my application's due in a few weeks."

"Why does this have to be part of it?" asked Nik. "What does this have to do with Rachel Riley, again?"

"Because," I explained, "all the kids who think Rachel burned down the barn think she did it as revenge for the game. And whoever made this website had to be one of the primary game players. They're probably one of the main bullies. Blake, or someone, but I can't really see him putting together a website. He had to ask Ms. Anyanwu, our computer teacher, how to do *copy and paste* the other day."

"Yikes."

"Yeah. So it's all a puzzle I'm trying to put together."

"Well, *this* piece is going to take this coder a few days, at least," Nik said. "But I'll work on it once I have time."

"Thanks." I turned to walk out of her room.

"Hey, Anna?"

"Yeah?" I glanced back at her.

"Have you been sleeping on my floor and then getting up before I wake up?"

I froze. "Um . . . occasionally." *If by "occasionally" you mean almost every night.* "I haven't been sleeping so good. It's too quiet here."

Nik just stared at me. Then she nodded. "Yeah. I know what you mean."

"You don't mind?"

"No. But I hope you get some sleep soon."

"Yeah," I told her. "Me too."

10

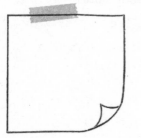

NOVEMBER 4

Jordan—

You can't stay mad at me forever. I'm really, really sorry for telling Anna. But she promised she wasn't going to do anything stupid, like tell Principal Howe or whatever. Nobody's going to find out. It will all be fine. Please talk to me!!!!

Xoxo

Kaylee

Kaylee,

It's ok. I wish you hadn't told her. I just like to pretend the whole "game" never happened. I don't like to think about it and I'm still so mad it ruined our dance. It's just like a big stupid stain on all of last year and I DON'T want it dragged into this one. That's all. I'm not mad anymore. Do you want to come over after school?

OxOx

Jordan

Jordan—

YAY ☺ I hate fighting. I will for sure come over. Let's stop and get shakes at Ella's Deli first??

Xoxo

Kaylee

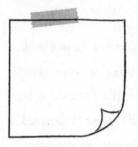

NOVEMBER 5

PERSONAL STATEMENT
RACHEL MARY RILEY

To Whom It May Concern,

My name is Rachel Riley, and this is my personal statement, as requested by the Moorland Academy of the Arts. I'm applying to attend your prestigious music school next fall as a ninth grader.

I've been playing the violin for eight years. I began as a student at the Wisconsin Conservatory of Music, then joined my public school's orchestra in fourth grade, which was the earliest possible opportunity. Since then, I've been fortunate enough to participate in fantastic groups like the Wisconsin

Youth Symphony Orchestra, as well as competing at the local level and winning the blue ribbon for the Youth Strings Grand Prix in 2021.

I could tell you about how much I love the violin—the way it sounds, the way it feels, even the way it smells when you first take it out of its case. But what I really want you to know is that music has been the one place I've been able to return to over and over when things in life have felt difficult. There have been times in my life, especially in the past year, when I have felt incredibly alone. School was the last place I wanted to be—except for that perfect thirty minutes when I could play the violin during orchestra. There, everything seemed to make sense.

Music means so much to me. That's why I want to spend all day, every day, practicing at Moorland Academy of the Arts. Thank you for your consideration.

Sincerely,
Rachel Riley

WISCONSIN STATE JOURNAL

JUNE 8, 2021
ACCESSED NOVEMBER 6

Study: Sexual Harassment Frequent
at the Middle School Level
By: Kinsley Culver

New research published Monday states that at least 1 in 4 middle school students report experiencing unwanted sexual harassment on school grounds.

Researchers from the University of Wisconsin-Madison surveyed nearly 10,000 students from 30 Midwestern middle schools. Overall, the numbers were staggering—26 percent of girls and 24 percent of boys reported experiencing verbal or physical sexual harassment in the hallways or classroom.

"These numbers are very distressing, but it was also interesting that so many students dismissed the incidents easily," said Sofia Lopez, a professor of educational psychology at the University of Wisconsin–Madison. "Although the number of students alone is alarming, what adds to our shock is how many students would simply say the unwanted physical or verbal attention was just a joke. At a young age, these kids are already normalizing sexual harassment."

Lopez went on to stress the importance of teachers and parents discussing healthy boundaries with their middle school–aged children.

"It's much more than putting a policy in a handbook. It's about conversation, implementation, and community," Lopez said.

LISTEN: THERE ARE PEOPLE IN THIS WORLD WHO ARE sporty. My dad is one of them. Give him any kind of ball, and he can get it through a goal or a hoop. He runs, too, in the mornings before we all wake up. Mom always says if you see her running, you better start running, too, because there's probably a grizzly bear or serial killer not far behind her. Nik and I have both adopted that philosophy.

That's why I hate gym. Gym teachers are so obsessed with physical fitness. But gym isn't *really* about fitness. It's about skill and competition, like how well you can dribble a ball or beat someone to a basket. How *fast* you can run. Things you can measure. Those kind of fitness things I've never been good at, no matter how hard I try. It's like they think they're going to create scholarship-winning athletes by making us all run in circles for a few minutes every day. Never mind the fact that there's a soda machine in every hallway. Like, *hello*. But I'm not *not* fit. I go on walks with my mom lots of nights, and I walk to and from school every day, and Dad cooks pretty healthy meals with lots of vegetables. At my yearly physical I always have normal blood pressure and a good heart rate.

But for weeks, we'd been preparing for run-the-mile day in gym class. The day we'd all have to run four sweaty laps around the track. We knew it would be in November, so as it crept closer, I was clinging to the possibility we'd get snowed out. But of course, on run-the-mile day, it was one of those freakishly warm fall days that make you think of global warming.

I'd actually asked to stay home that day. Dentist appointment, *anything*. But Dad reminded me that life is full of Hard Things, and having to do hard things in school was just the beginning.

"If you avoid all of your problems, you'll never be able to handle adulthood," Dad said, pointing his spatula at me. At least he made blueberry waffles. Carb loading—one small perk. "You'll become a person who calls the police on people letting their dogs off leash in public parks. Who has a breakdown about bad traffic. Who can't handle *life*, you know?"

"If you have parents who will get you out of tough things at school, then one day you'll also try to have your parents call your boss when you're having a hard time at work," Mom said, pulling on her heels.

"I have parents of my law students emailing me about their kids' homework load. I mean, these are *adults*, here."

"The mile thing is kind of dumb. I agree," Dad said. "But doing kind-of-dumb things is part of life. Even in eighth grade."

"*Especially* in eighth grade," Nik said, pouring more syrup on her stack.

So I surrendered. But two weird things happened in gym class that day. Actually, three, now that I think about it. All of the girls in the locker room were talking about bras, because we had a Bra Emergency in our midst. And really, that's where it all started.

"I forgot my sports bra," said Chelsea, digging through her backpack. "I know right where it is, too. In the dryer at home. I can just *see* it." And she seemed *panicked*. She probably had every right to be. She was one of the girls in our class who actually needed a bra. I wore one just so that I didn't feel like a baby.

"Crap," said Jordan. "I'm sorry. I had an extra in here, but I just took it home yesterday to get it washed."

"It's gonna be so uncomfortable," said Chelsea. "And I'm going to be . . . bouncing."

We kind of giggled, until we realized Chelsea *wasn't* giggling. At all.

"You could just wear a sweatshirt, maybe?" suggested Bee.

"I know Kaylee's gym locker combination," said Jordan. Kaylee wasn't in our gym class; she had it in the afternoon. "I could see if her sports bra is in there. She wouldn't care if you borrowed it."

"I'll stretch it out . . ." said Chelsea nervously. But she didn't stop Jordan, who quickly checked Kaylee's gym locker. But all that was in there was a pair of socks, an empty tube of ChapStick, and—

A pack of bright green hall passes. What the heck were those doing in her locker? Weird Thing Number One: there was no way a student was supposed to have a pack of passes. The other girls were so distracted by the bra issue that they didn't even notice. And for some reason, I reached out and took them. I had no idea why. But I slid them right into my backpack.

"You know, there are girls all over the world who don't even *have* bras," Elizabeth said. Her other half wasn't in our gym class, so the rest of us were usually subject to her speeches on various injustices of the world. "Tampons, too. It's a huge reason why so many girls don't go to school. In fact—"

"Girls!" Coach Hoffman banged on the locker-room door. "You're about to get points docked! We need to hustle up and get out there!"

"I'll just have to suck it up," she groaned. But the gym T-shirt she pulled on was a white UW T-shirt, and you could definitely see her bright aqua bra right under it. She crossed her arms.

"Do you want my sweatshirt?" Bee offered. "I have it . . ."

"Nah. I'll sweat, and then I'll stink, and everyone will be asking *why* I'm wearing a sweatshirt," said Chelsea.

We hurried outside. Carmen and Lia did their thing, complaining about their periods. I'm not sure if Coach Hoffman had gone his entire life without attending a health class or if he just didn't want to be the male teacher who accused two girls of fake-menstruating, but he always just let them sit stuff out every week, and this was no different. They skipped off to the weight room for "exercise," and I rolled my eyes at my lazy, non-period-having uterus. That plus my inability to lie to teachers was going to equal a rough gym class.

When Coach Hoffman yelled, "Go," and hit his little timer, we took off. This is where things got embarrassing. My feet were flopping everywhere, my sides were pounding, and I couldn't keep my arms straight. I was out of breath *so* fast. I legiti-mately thought I was going to have a heart attack.

I don't know how Jordan and Riz and tons of other people can just rip around the track four times like they're out for a leisurely jog. I started walking the corners on my very second lap, and I was starting to feel sorry for myself when I remembered what Mom had said that morning, after Dad's big Hard Things in Life talk: that nobody will ever mention how fast someone could run the mile at a person's funeral. So whatever. I kept run-walk-run-walking, and finally panted across the finish line. My time was pathetic, and I was covered in sweat.

Then, the second weird thing happened. Blake Wyatt—burping, bumping-into-things, slapping-girls-on-the-butt-and-keeping-score, backward-baseball-cap-and-bad-attitude-having Blake Wyatt—high-fived me.

"Good job," he said. And it almost felt like he *meant* it. He'd *double* lapped me. But he was smiling at me, nice, and it was—like he was trying to be kind. And when the very last kid crossed the finish line—Angela Williams, who, because of a disability, was able to walk the entire thing with an aide and didn't get timed—Blake did the same thing. A high five. A nice smile. A "Good job."

And I was thinking about that *good job*, that small bread crumb of kindness, when the third weird thing happened. After we ran the mile, we went back into the gym and got to have free time the rest of class. Some people picked up basketballs and started playing HORSE, but most of us just sat on the bleachers and talked. There were only about five minutes left in class when Chelsea hopped up to get a drink at the water fountain. Jordan and Bee and Elizabeth were deep in conversation about some new Netflix show that I didn't watch, so I was just zoning out a little. Looking around. And I saw it—Carlos Agnelli, with his floppy brown hair, running behind her, acting like he was running toward a basketball. Leaning forward and—

Grabbing that bright turquoise bra strap right through her T-shirt. Snapping it.

She turned around, her face a million shades of red, and Carlos tried to hide a smile as he jogged back toward Blake and Riz and Trevor and Cody. They were all cracking up, and Blake, Mr. Good-Job-Nice-Guy, gave him a fist bump.

"Five points, at least," said Carlos. His voice echoed loud through the gym, but Coach Hoffman was in his office, writing down our mile times. We were alone. "Extra because it's *Chelsea*." Who knew what the heck that meant? Because Chelsea had big boobs, or because Chelsea wore blue bras, or *what*?

"Five points," agreed Blake, laughing.

I turned back to the girls. I felt like I couldn't breathe all of a sudden. I thought nobody had witnessed what happened, but then I noticed Jordan looking at Chelsea. She'd seen. I could tell. I looked back at Chelsea, who looked like she was going to cry. She didn't even come back to the group. She ran into the locker room.

Nobody followed her.

I should have. I know that. I should have gotten off my butt and walked my two legs back into that locker room to make sure she was okay. You can know the *should* of a moment, but you can also choose not to go through with it. Instead, I found myself grabbing Jordan's arm.

"You saw that," I whispered.

Jordan yanked her arm away. "Saw what?"

"Jordan . . . she's—she's your friend."

"What's that supposed to mean?" she asked. She sounded *mad*. I didn't know Jordan Russell very well, but I'd never seen her mad. Not even when Kaylee accidentally spilled an entire jar of water on one of her paintings in art class.

"We have to do something," I said. I felt my voice getting louder in the echoey gym.

"Why are you freaking out? It's just their game.

Their stupid game that they played all last year. I know you know all about it," she whispered back. "Kaylee *told* me she told you. So that's all they're doing. Don't be dramatic."

"She looked really upset," I said.

"She'll be fine," said Jordan. And her voice had a sense of *that's it* to it. Like, *I am done with this conversation now.* She turned back toward the other girls.

She'll be fine. Well, she would be. She would *have* to be, because what was the alternative? Not asking boys to not snap bra straps, apparently. It was just who they were, Kaylee had said. Playing these games. Snapping bra straps, slapping butts. Taking moments of dignity away, piece by piece. Taking, just because they *wanted*, like Nik said. A nice moment followed by a mean moment. A *good job, high five* smile followed by a *five points* fist bump.

She should have known. Don't walk around at night by yourself. Don't wear a blue bra. It reminded me of when we lived back in Chicago and Dad's truck was broken into. They took his GPS, his stereo system, all of it—just pulled it all out of the car. *My fault,* he said. He forgot to lock it. He was so comfortable in our little neighborhood, with the twenty-four-hour gas station across the street. His fault for not locking his car. For not keeping his guard up. But just because you forget to lock your car, do you deserve to lose your stereo system? Does that become your fault? We lock our cars because we're told to assume nothing is safe, that the world is full of robbers. But it's tiring to walk through a world assuming your stereo could be gone in an instant. And that if it is, it was probably your fault. A robber wants, and a robber takes.

Well, joke was on the robber. They took the ancient CD player, and that thing had a Jimmy Buffett album in it. Hope they knew the way to Margaritaville.

We could say it was because of a blue bra with a white T-shirt, but it wasn't. It was because Carlos wanted, so Carlos took.

11

Join Global Leaders!

Are you passionate about making the world a better place?

Global Leaders meets in room 912 Wednesdays after school.

Contact Elizabeth at

ebaker@east.middle.edu

for more information.

NOVEMBER 9

HI, MS. O'DELL. YOU ASKED US TO MAKE A RECORDING talking about someone we admire in our local community, and someone we admire that would be considered a well-known world changer. So here's mine.

A well-known world changer that I admire is Mimi Miller. She's a podcaster. I love the way she isn't afraid to ask hard questions and get to know the truth behind issues. She's balanced, too—she interviews people who think all different things.

Someone local was harder, though. To be honest, I didn't even know the name of the mayor. I had to google it. Sorry—I'm guessing a Social Issues teacher is pretty disappointed in that. But it's true! Maybe Mimi Miller should interview him, ha. Then I'd remember.

And then I thought of someone I really admire. You! I'm not just saying that to get a good grade. I just really like your class. It's fun to talk about real-world issues, but not feel like we have to have all the answers. I like that you let everyone talk, even when people disagree, and that we sit in a big circle instead of rows. I like that you actually care about our opinions, even though you went to college and know so much more than us, probably. You're probably my favorite teacher I've ever had.

Actually, now that I say it all together like this . . . you're a lot like Mimi Miller. I guess local figures can be world changers, too, even if they're not big or well-known. I mean, didn't Martin Luther King Jr. and Susan B. Anthony and Mimi Miller probably have teachers that changed *their* worlds? And then they changed other people's worlds?

Wait—was that the point of this? To get us to recognize that?

See? You *are* a good teacher!

NOVEMBER 9

Anna: This is WHAT HAPPENED TO RACHEL RILEY?: AN INVESTIGATION BY ANNA HUNT. *I'm here today with Rachel herself, who has agreed to talk to us on the record.*

Rachel: Only because of what I saw after algebra.

Anna: Can you explain what that was to the phone? I mean, to Mimi Miller? I mean, to our audience?

<silence>

Anna: I'm new at this. I have to work out some of the kinks.

Rachel: Clearly. Anyway . . . what I saw was Blake Wyatt snap Kaylee's bra strap.

Anna: Kaylee Nakamura, one of our earlier interviewees.

Rachel: You got Kaylee to talk to you? That's surprising. She's kind of prickly. Nice, though. Most of the time.

Anna: Funny for someone to say who's been bullied the entire year. I mean, she doesn't seem that nice.

Rachel: Yeah, well, lots of people aren't what they seem.

Anna: So, how did you feel seeing the latest iteration of the butt-slap game?

Rachel: Who told you about that?

Anna: My sources are anonymous.

Rachel: Anna. Come on.

Anna: Do you want me telling everyone else what you say on here?

Rachel: Okay, fine. Fine. What was the question? How I felt about it? How do you think I felt about it?

Anna: I don't know. That's why I'm asking.

Rachel: Well, you should know. I hate it now, and I hated it last year. Everyone hated it.

Anna: My source said it was mostly a joke. That you were the only one who got that upset about it.

Rachel: Your source is wrong. We all hated it. But if you got mad, you made it worse. Then they'd really target you. That's what happened to me. Most people just pretended they didn't care, because they didn't want to be the new . . . well, me.

Anna: What do you mean?

Rachel: One day—I can't believe I'm telling you this. Okay, so, the first time Blake did it, I got kind of mad. Kaylee and Jordan were just laughing, but, like, it wasn't funny to me. Come on. We're supposed to be feminists, aren't we? Marching in the streets. Not letting boys just . . . do whatever they want. But I didn't want to be a jerk, either, so I kind of laughed, and told Blake to stop. I meant it. But maybe I didn't sound like I meant it.

Anna: And what'd he do?

Rachel: What'd he do? Laughed even harder. Told me not to freak out. Told the other guys I was super dramatic. And you know what happened next? Points doubled for me. My butt was getting slapped all day, every day. Every time I went in the hallway. I mean—Jesus. I don't like talking about this.

<silence>

Anna: Are you okay? Should I turn it off?

Rachel: Yeah. No.

Anna: We could take a break . . .

Rachel: No. No, it's fine. It's—well, it's not fine, you know? It's not fine. I couldn't do anything. I felt completely—powerless. That's such a dramatic word, but it's how I felt. Trapped and powerless.

Anna: I don't blame you.

Rachel: I mean, I had it bad. So did Jordan. They've always had it out for her, because she's so pretty, and it's Jordan, so she'd never yell at them or anything. She's, like, the nicest human who's ever set foot on planet Earth. So I didn't even bother telling them to stop again, because I knew it would just make it worse on me. She got it bad because she did nothing. I got it bad because I did something.

Anna: Did you tell any teachers or anything?

Rachel: Ha. No. They wouldn't help.

Anna: How do you know?

Rachel: Because. Because I just know. The year before, back in sixth grade, this guy had a huge crush on me. Kyle Walsh. He moved away that summer. But he smelled bad, and wore sweatshirts all year round. Maybe I sound like a jerk. I don't mean to. I try to be like Jordan—nice to everybody. But he creeped me out. And he had anger issues, too. One time in English he got so frustrated trying to read aloud, because he wasn't good at it, that he kicked his desk over and ran out of the room. He would do things like that. He once got in trouble at lunch for looking at something weird on his phone and showing it to all the guys.

Anna: Sounds like he should have creeped you out.

Rachel: Right? But he liked me. A lot. He'd leave notes in my locker and always try to sit by me. He started trying to hold my hand in the halls. I got so— just, uncomfortable, that I told my math teacher, Mrs. Kang. And you know what she said?

Anna: What?

Rachel: That I wasn't being kind. That he obviously had troubles at home, and he liked me, so I should be nice to him or just ignore him. Apparently, his right to creep me out was more important than my right to not be creeped out. Apparently, him trying to hold my hand was kind and me saying no was not kind. So no. I don't trust teachers. And if you want my opinion, nobody should. Plus, Mr. Corey—the art teacher?

Anna: Yeah?

Rachel: He saw it once. Not me. But he saw Riz slap Chelsea's butt. And Chelsea laughed, and so did Riz—and so did Mr. Corey.

Anna: That's . . . messed up.

Rachel: You know who you can depend on in this school? This whole stupid world? Your very own self. And that's about it.

Anna: So, what are you going to do now? I mean, about what you saw outside of algebra?

Rachel: I'll think of something.

<bell rings>

Rachel: I'm sorry, Anna. I'm sorry that you picked this project. I'm sorry you have to go to this stupid school.

Anna: Wait—I have one more question.

Rachel: I have to go.

Anna: Is that why you did it? Is that why you burned down the barn?

Rachel: It was an accident. The barn was an accident. I told my parents, and I told the police, and I'm telling you.

Anna: But . . . if telling them to stop was so pointless, if it made everything so much worse, why did you leave a note in Blake's locker the next day? Threatening to report them . . . but you just said you didn't trust the teachers to do anything.

Rachel: I—I changed my mind, I guess.

Anna: Wait—did you leave the note? Or was it someone else?

Rachel: Goodbye, Anna.

Official Sexual Harassment Policy from the East Middle School Handbook

East Middle School prohibits any form of sexual harassment by all persons within the school district, including, but not limited to, students and staff. This policy applies to conduct during and related to the operation of East Middle School.

Harassment will not be tolerated under any circumstance. "Sexual harassment" is defined here as repetitive unwelcome behavior of a sexual nature that creates an intimidating or hostile educational environment or interferes with an individual's work or academic performance.

East Middle School will take all necessary steps to put an end to sexual harassment of anyone in school and at school-sponsored activities.

THE WEEK FLEW BY, AND BY SATURDAY, I WANTED TO stay in my bed the entire day. It sounded like a pretty good plan—a warm cocoon of blankets, my laptop with some *Great British Baking Show* queued up, maybe an adventure to the kitchen for some tea. It was cold and gray outside. It looked like how I felt: tired. *Exhausted*, really. Partly because I was up so late most nights, in the creepy quiet of the dark and silence. I still tiptoed to Nik's room around 3:00 a.m. and eventually fell asleep on her floor, but I always got back to my own room by the time Mom and Dad were up.

It was more than that, too. More than a physical tired. An *inner* tired. All of this Rachel Riley stuff, and the game at school, Carlos and that blue bra strap—it was wearing me out. I could barely concentrate in my other classes. I was tired of thinking about Heavy Things.

Mom and Dad had big plans. Some pottery store in Cambridge.

"You gonna stay in here all day, lazy girl?" Mom asked, glancing around my room. It wasn't even eight a.m. yet, but Hunts were early risers.

"It's the weekend," I reminded her. "I'm a growing adolescent."

"I just took the dogs out, but don't forget to take them out again in a couple of hours, okay?" Mom said. "A walk might be good, too. Kix seems all riled up." Kix *always* seemed all riled up. If Jesse had pinkies, they'd always be up, but Kix was more like one of those people who can eat thirty hot dogs in under a minute.

I heard them say goodbye to Nik, then shoved myself deeper into my cocoon. But almost as soon as the front door shut, my sister was knocking on my door.

"What?" I yelled.

She popped her head in. "I'm making pancakes. You hungry?"

"Chocolate chips?"

"Duh."

I stumbled downstairs in my sweats, and Nik got out the griddle. Kix immediately started running laps around the kitchen like he was training for the Olympics, and Jesse gave us a lazy howl of acknowledgment.

"Yeah, yeah. Some for you two dingbats, too. Sans chocolate chips," Nik said. She loved those dogs as much as I did. As much as we *all* did. Dogs had a big job, taking care of families. Giving them snuggles when they needed it and being something cute to look at. You could talk and talk and talk, and a dog would just listen. They didn't ask for anything but your leftovers and the occasional belly rub. And how many people only got exercise because they had to take their dogs for walks?

I didn't want to talk about Rachel Riley, but I couldn't help it. It was all I could think about.

"Did you make any progress on who BilboBaggins1201 is?" I asked.

"No, sorry. I had a math test Friday that took up a ton of my time. Plus, CodeHERs. I'll look into it more this week."

"I can't believe you joined a club," I said, getting out the butter and syrup. Nutella, too. Go big or go home.

"What's so wrong with a club?" she asked. "Lots of people are in clubs. And besides, it's not a *club*. It's a mentorship program."

Nik had a new look of purpose here. In this city and this house. She had the same curly brown hair from Dad, shoved into the same messy knot on top of her head. The same blue eyes we all had. But she just seemed a little more shiny, like she was getting more sun. She was nicer, too—she bit less, like a puppy that had gone to training school. Nik hadn't had any friends in Chicago except Mom, Dad, and me, but can you really count the sister you're forced to share a room with as your friend?

"Nothing," I said. "Nothing."

"How's the rest of the ole eighth grade going?" she asked. She flipped our pancakes, and the griddle sizzled. "Now that I actually have a life, Mom and Dad are worried about *you*. I heard them the other night. They wish you felt more excited about the winter dance. Mom was saying she was gonna ask you if you wanted to have some girls over for a sleepover afterward."

I shrugged. "I have people to talk to."

"But do you have *friends*?"

"Like you should talk," I snapped. "Your best friend last year was *Call of Duty*."

In Chicago, Nik would have stormed off, but now she just laughed. "Yeah, well, I joined the world a little bit here. And it feels nice. You should try it."

"You're just saying that because you have a *boyfriend*," I sang.

She didn't say anything, but her cheery exterior

seemed to fall. Her eyes zoned out for a minute. I felt a little bad for bringing him up. I was trying to be funny, but she didn't even crack a smile.

"He's not my boyfriend," she said flatly. "He's really starting to bug me, actually."

"How?"

"Just—still won't stop texting me. Whatever. It's fine." She flipped our pancakes onto a plate. "He'll get the hint eventually."

"Well . . . I *do* have friends," I said. "Kind of. But you know that creepy butt-slap game?" We walked over to the living room and fell onto the couch. No kitchen table and chairs for us. Dad would lose it if we got syrup on the couch. We'd have to be careful.

"Yeah?"

"It's back. But it's different."

"What do you mean?"

"It's bra straps instead of butts. I saw it in gym on Friday. Carlos did it to Chelsea. Plus, afterward, too—after algebra, Blake did it to Kaylee."

Nik stopped eating. She put her fork down on her plate, and I actually remember the sound—the *clink* of the fork hitting the plate.

"Anna. *God.*"

"Our Father, who art in Heaven . . ." I nodded toward the crucifix hanging over our front door.

"I'm not *joking*! Did she tell them to stop?"

"She didn't exactly call 911."

Nik shook her head. "Anna, not good. You have to tell somebody."

"Look. I wouldn't like it, either. And people didn't like it—*don't* like it. It's all a joke, *haha*, but when it happens—you should see their faces. Hear them talk about it after the fact. But why is it on the girls? Why is it just expected that *we'll* be the ones to say something and get all mad? Why can't we just depend on boys to *not* slap butts and snap bra straps?!"

"Because. You can't depend on people to not do *bad*. You can only depend on yourself to do *good*. You have to rely on your own self." She sounded like Rachel.

"Well, it's hard to be good!" I snapped. I set my plate down on the coffee table, hard. I was angry now, too. Angry about Blake and Carlos, yeah, but more than that: angry at Edgar Allan Poe.

I learned in English that when Edgar Allan Poe was twenty-seven, he married a *thirteen-year-old*. Charles Dickens, too—Mom once watched a documentary on him. He left his wife for an eighteen-year-old. Pablo Picasso was forty-five when he cheated on *his* wife with a seventeen-year-old—that was in a show Babcia told me about.

Angry for girls in the world, all the way to the

beginning of time. The women in the *Bible*, for God's sake—literally. You want to hear about female *oppression*? Start with the oldest book in the universe.

And I felt like I could just see it—this line, all the way from the men stoning the woman in the Bible to Edgar Allan Poe to Blake Wyatt and Carlos Agnelli. All of that heavy responsibility, on *our* shoulders, when it shouldn't be. It was hard to always have to be so aware of your surroundings and the color of your underwear.

I stormed upstairs. The dogs could eat my pancakes; I didn't care. I heard Nik scrape my plate into their bowl, and they went at it like they hadn't eaten in weeks. I got back into my bed and fell asleep, the kind of deep sleep where you aren't even dreaming. When I woke up a few hours later, Nik was sitting on my bed. She was looking out the window. It was still wet and gray.

"Sorry to wake you up," she said.

"Oh my gosh. I needed that nap."

"I told you, everything works better when you unplug it for a while. Even people, right? Ha. Mom and Dad are grabbing lunch in Cambridge," she said. "They won't be back for a while."

I just nodded and turned over. The good thing about sisters: apologies can hang there in the air.

They don't always need to be said. You let each other freak out, and you just kind of deal. Nik sat there, and the weight of her on my bed felt right. I didn't want to be alone.

"A person can feel powerless," I said. Rachel's word; her dramatic word that didn't feel so dramatic.

She nodded. "It makes you feel little, you know? Not little, like young, just small. Smaller than oceans and mountains and these big, stupid problems."

"It shouldn't be like this."

"I know you wish the world were a fair place, Anna," Nik said quietly. "But sometimes, it just doesn't work that way. Sometimes, fairness has to be demanded instead of waited for."

⇒ 12 ⇐

NOVEMBER 13

To: Katarzyna Kowalski <babciakat@gmail.com>
From: Anna Hunt <ahunt@east.middle.edu>
Subj: Ugh

Babcia,

You said in your email that it's not about not knowing who I am. It's about *becoming* who I am, and that that's a process people do every day. That *you're* still doing it.

But when do we get to just wake up and know ourselves? That's what I want to know. When do you just get to wake up and feel confident about your decisions? Some people seem like they feel so sure of themselves. Mom: tough lawyer who can wear high heels and recite the Constitution. Nik: smart coder who could start a revolution with a few keystrokes. Dad: lawyer with a boring job and a knack for making perfectly crispy bacon. When I think of *Anna*, it's a blank space.

I guess to become who you are, it's all of the little choices you make every single day. But what if the choices you're making aren't the right ones? Who are you then?

I liked your penguin fact. I'll make sure to use it in my report. You don't think of penguins as having camouflage, like chameleons or something. But it made sense when you explained that the white reflects from underneath and the black blends in from above. Sometimes, I wish I could put on a big old penguin suit. I know everyone at school loves to share every second of their lives on Instagram, but eighth grade might be a whole lot easier if nobody were *looking*.

Love,
Anna

NOVEMBER 14

To: Anna Hunt <ahunt@east.middle.edu>

CC: Malika Jones <mjones@east.middle.edu>

From: Elizabeth Baker <ebaker@east.middle.edu>

Subj: Re: Sexual Harassment at East

Anna,

I was really surprised to get your email since we've been trying to recruit you for Global Leaders all year long! That being said, what you're talking about isn't really what we do here. We're more focused on *global* issues. It's important for us to concentrate on things affecting the planet and people all over the world. Not Blake Wyatt being annoying. That's more the guidance counselor, Dr. Fayen's, lane than ours.

Come to a meeting anytime to learn more—we'd love to have you.

From,

Elizabeth, founder and president of Global Leaders

(And Malika, cofounder and copresident)

NIK AND I HAD DECIDED THE DAY BEFORE: I WOULD ask the Global Leaders girls if this was something *they* would tackle. So I was doing something, but not having to get involved. I wrote my email on Sunday night, explaining it to Elizabeth-and-Malika. What I'd seen, and what was happening. I said that maybe we needed an update to the sexual harassment policy. I said that someone needed to *do* something.

And so getting that email ticked me off. Elizabeth-and-Malika seemed like they cared so much—about pollution, and violence, and forest fires. Pamphlets and fundraisers and stands in the cafeteria. Matching T-shirts for the issue of the week. But there was an issue *right here*, and they didn't want to get involved in it? There was a problem right in front of their faces they could actually make a real difference in, and they were just going to do nothing?

I wondered, as I walked past Brocach Irish Pub and Trader Joe's on my way home from school, if it was easier to care about people you didn't actually know than the people right in front of you. Heck, if it was easier to care about people you didn't actually know than *yourself*—that felt true, for sure. You could care without it affecting you, in a way. Writing a check, or gathering shoes . . . those things were so much easier than actually talking to another person. Or learning how they got to where they are.

I took the long way because I just wasn't in the mood to go home yet. Winter was here, knocking at the door, like it always did in the Midwest. Too early. The rest of the world was pulling out sweatshirts and jackets while we were gearing up with snowblowers. It was getting dark earlier and earlier. But I took my time. It felt good to get some fresh air. Father Andrew was sweeping the leaves off the steps of Sacred Heart, and we waved at each other. I wove in between some Atwood Avenue streets, and then I passed the little ice cream stand on the corner of Bluemound and Moorland—Lee's Dairy Emporium.

When most kids wanted ice cream, they'd go to Ella's Deli, with its cool carousel and cheese fries. I'd only lived here for a few months, and even I'd already figured that out. But Lee's Dairy Emporium was small and simple—only a few flavors and three tables inside, plus soft serve. It usually looked pretty empty.

And then I saw them. Sitting inside, at a table together—Cody McLeen and Rachel Riley.

Rachel looked upset about something. She was telling him something, and he was looking down at his feet, nodding. Then she got up, pulled on her backpack, and tossed an empty Styrofoam bowl in the garbage before leaving.

Crap! She was going to see me. But it's not like there was anywhere to hide. I stood frozen still—if it were a movie, it would have worked, and she would have walked right by me. But it was real life. So when she came out of the door, she just stared at me.

"Anna," she said.

"Hey," I replied.

She glanced back at Cody and opened her mouth as if she was going to say something. But then she just sighed, closed her mouth again, and shook her head before walking right past me.

When my eyes returned to Cody, he was looking right at me.

I pulled open the door and went in. The little bells jingled, but the tall teenager behind the counter didn't even look up from his phone. The shop smelled sticky sweet, like chocolate syrup.

"Hey, Mr. Not-Friends-with-Rachel," I said.

He shrugged. "Hey, New Girl with the Weird Project."

"You lied to me."

"I guess so," he said. He didn't even seem like he felt bad.

"You're not a very good friend if you're embarrassed to say you're someone's friend," I said. "Your mom *told* me you guys used to be best friends."

"My *mom*?"

"She's planning the winter dance with my mom," I said.

He just blinked at me. "Did it ever occur to you that *I'm* not the one who doesn't want people to know we're friends?"

What? That didn't make any sense. Why wouldn't Rachel want at least one friend? Especially one she'd known forever? Those forever friends—I've always wanted one of those. My Chicago friends, Kateri and Sabrina . . . we hadn't really been like that. I had Nik. I guess it was kind of the same thing. She didn't always like me, though. It kind of depended on her mood.

"Look," he said, "it's just . . . easier this way. Okay? Easier for both of us. Rachel knew what she was getting into. Besides, she only has one year to deal with this."

"Till middle school's over, and we go to high school?" I asked. It was true. All the kids from West would filter into our high school, too. It could be a fresh start.

Cody nodded. "Yeah, but she won't even be at our high school probably, right? So who cares if they all hate her now?"

"Why won't she be at our high school? Is she moving?"

"She's auditioning for Moorland. The big fancy arts school on the lake? It's a high school for musicians and actors and artists and stuff. She plays the violin. She's *incredible*. Rachel will get in for sure. She's wanted to go there since we were little kids. It's why she does all of these private lessons and stuff. And then she can put this whole stupid year behind her."

"Like in *The Way to Stay in Destiny*?" I asked, without thinking. "Oh—sorry. That's a book."

"I know," he said, annoyed. "I've read it."

"You have?" I asked, surprised. I'd never seen him with a book in his hands at school.

"I like to read," he snapped. "And no. That was a dancing school. This is a school-school, just with a music focus."

Cody looked like the other guys—tall, skinny.

Floppy blond hair. Some acne. No braces, like Blake or Carlos. And he hung out with all of those guys, too. But something about him just seemed kind of different. I could see why he and Rachel were friends.

"Anyway," he said, "I don't think we *are* friends anymore. Rachel's mad at me."

"Why?"

"None of your business. I don't even know you. You—you've got a lot of nerve, you know? Just showing up and acting like you have a right to know all of our personal stuff?"

"I'm just trying to help. Help someone who's *your* friend," I told him. "Nobody deserves to be treated the way Rachel's treated."

"That, I agree with," he said. "But you're not helping, okay? So cool it." He stood up, grabbing his backpack. "I need to go. My mom's making me help her fold invitations for this stupid winter dance."

I turned to go.

"Anna. Wait. Don't tell anyone you saw us here, okay?" he said. "As far as Rachel's concerned, we're never speaking again. So it doesn't matter, anyway."

I just nodded, even though I wasn't sure if I'd keep that promise.

"We're not a project, okay, new girl? We're *people*," he said.

Cody pushed back from the table and stood, grabbing his jacket. He quickly bolted, letting the door slam behind him. With he and Rachel gone, I changed my mind and decided to stay. I suddenly needed sugar—badly. Sitting in a quiet ice cream shop with a scoop and *A Great and Terrible Beauty* sounded like the perfect way to spend the next half hour. I wanted to read about girls at a fancy British boarding school, not think about Rachel Riley. I texted Dad that I would be home a little late and pulled out my wallet.

"Can I get a scoop of Oreo?" I asked the teenager.

He nodded and typed a code into his register. Something *ding-ding-ding*ed.

"Whoa," he said. "You're our hundredth customer this week."

"Um . . . cool."

"No, it means you get a gift card. Here." He pulled out a card and beeped it with his scanner. "Twenty bucks. Lucky you."

"Yeah," I said. "Lucky me."

13

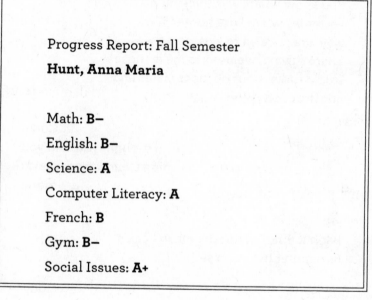

Progress Report: Fall Semester
Hunt, Anna Maria

Math: **B–**
English: **B–**
Science: **A**
Computer Literacy: **A**
French: **B**
Gym: **B–**
Social Issues: **A+**

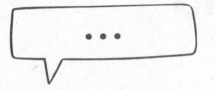

NOVEMBER 16

:

You know what I was thinking of
yesterday when I got home? The
way when we were kids, and it was
Thanksgiving, we used to make those
stupid turkeys out of paper plates and
construction paper.

> Cody:
> I thought you said you
> didn't want to be friends
> anymore.

:

I don't. But that doesn't mean I can't
remember the good stuff.

> Cody:
> No, but I wish it meant
> you wouldn't tell me
> about it.

:

Okay. Sorry.

NOVEMBER 16

To: Maja Hunt <mhunt@wisc.edu>
From: Lana McLeen <lana@lanamcleen.com>
Subj: To Do List—winter dance

Maja,

Here's the list we agreed on for winter dance prep! Thanks to your help, this is going to be one of the most spectacular soirees East Middle School has ever thrown.

To Do—Lana

- Send out invitations
- Hire DJ—go over CLEAN music list
- Check on AV setup
- Décor—streamers, balloons, lights

To Do—Maja

- Gift bags (homemade cookies*, heart tattoos, gift certificate to school store)
- Coordinate parent volunteers . . . we need at least 12
- Purchase napkins, paper cups, and tablecloths

*For the cookies, remember that they need to be nut-free, sugar-free, gluten-free, and dairy-free, with no artificial dyes in the frosting!

Xo

Lana McLeen

Wedding Queen

www.lanamcleen.com

Reach out about YOUR event TODAY!

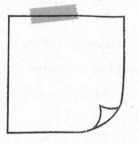

NOVEMBER 17

Jordan—

Do you want to come over before the dance Saturday night? My mom said I could have a few girls over to get ready. We can order Chinese food or something and take pictures.

Xoxo

Kaylee

Kaylee—

For sure! Do you know what you're wearing yet? I got a new dress from Macy's. My mom tried to make me wear this floral thing she found online. It was so weird, lol. The one I ended up getting is all shimmery and purple and cute. I'm so pumped.

OxOx

Jordan

Jordan—

OMG! Show me pics at lunch. I have to wear one of my sister's hand-me-downs, which is annoying, but she did wear it to homecoming last year, so it's pretty cute and kind of grown-up. It's black . . . is that too goth?

Xoxo

Kaylee

Kaylee—

No! It's sophisticated. Mom thinks mine makes me look like I'm "going out for happy hour," lol. Like that's an insult or something!!! Who do you want to dance with?

OxOx

Jordan

Jordan—

Idk . . . maybe Carlos? Who do YOU want to dance with??

Xoxo

Kaylee

Kaylee—

I don't want to dance with anybody, lol. All of the boys are annoying. I can't wait till we're in high school and can go to homecoming with MATURE boys!

OxOx

Jordan

NOVEMBER 18

This is WHAT HAPPENED TO RACHEL RILEY?: AN INVESTIGATION BY ANNA HUNT. *At this point, I have way more questions than answers.*

Like who left that note in Blake's locker the day after the fire?

Was it Rachel or someone else?

Who's trying to help me by leaving me notes in my locker?

And then there're all these other pieces that might be connected, but might not. Why did Kaylee have an entire pack of passes in her locker? Why doesn't Rachel want to be Cody's friend anymore, if he's the only person still being nice to her? And who made the butt-slap website?

I know, I know—it's like my Social Issues teacher always says. A good question doesn't always lead to answers—sometimes it just leads to more questions. If that's true, I'm asking very, very good questions.

NOVEMBER 18

Anna:
Can I ask you another
question for my project

Kaylee:
Yeah, but I'm not promising I'll
answer . . .

Anna:
Why did you have a pack
of passes in your gym
locker?

Kaylee:
YOU stole those?! What were you doing
in my locker??? That has nothing to do
with your project

Anna:
I'm sorry. It's a long story.
Jordan opened your locker for
something in gym and I just saw
them. I was just wondering why.

Kaylee:
OK, I'll tell you. Whatever. I don't care anymore. I took them as a favor for a friend. She had to cut class one day. Mr. Corey just left them in him top drawer where anyone can grab them.

Anna:
Mr. Corey, the art teacher?

Kaylee:
Yeah.

Anna:
Which friend?

Kaylee:
Like I said, it doesn't have to do with the project!!! Jordan just had something to do in the library one afternoon. It was career day and all she would miss was a boring assembly. Cody's mom was there with all her wedding décor, lol. It's not like she skipped a test or something.

Kaylee:
You're not going to tell on us are you?

Kaylee:
Hello?

Kaylee:
Anna!!!!

"I CAN'T BELIEVE I GOT SUCKED INTO THIS." MOM WAS sitting at the kitchen table, surrounded by sparkly purple gift bags, and Kix was happily lapping up the crumbs at her feet. Dad was grabbing dinner with some coworkers, and our kitchen still smelled like Culver's fries from the fast food Mom, Nik, and I had scarfed down.

"Whoa. Being Santa's helper? It's a little early," I said, plopping down at the kitchen table. My focus on the Rachel Riley project had resulted in my grades being—well, fine, but "fine" wasn't good enough for my parents, especially when they were used to me always getting straight As. Which meant I now had to report to the kitchen table every night after dinner to do homework and study or they'd start bugging me about how B-minuses wouldn't get me into UW one day.

"Lana," said Mom, rolling her eyes. "I swear, at St. Patrick's, I never had to do this rah-rah parent volunteer stuff."

"That's because it was Catholic school. We paid

tuition," I reminded her. "They *hired* people to plan school events."

"Yeah, well, do they know that my consulting fee is three hundred dollars an hour?" groaned Mom. "I should send them an invoice. I mean, I asked Lana if I could just *buy* the cookies for the gift bags. Support a local bakery—come on! I thought it was a no-brainer. And she said that a *homemade touch* is what really makes events *sparkle*."

"All hail the Wedding Queen."

"Some women bake the cookies, some women teach about the Constitution. I'm the latter."

"Hey. Some women do both," I pointed out.

"You're right! But I'm not one of them. I've got your dad on cookie-baking duty this weekend," Mom admitted. "In the nation of the Hunt household, baking is an equal-opportunity activity."

"Plus, you always eat so much dough we barely have any left for the cookies."

"Listen, I know they tell you not to eat the raw eggs, but what's life without a little risk?" She pushed away the silver spool of ribbon she'd been using to tie the baggies. "Break time." She grabbed the giant pile of mail we'd been letting grow on the counter and started sorting it into piles. "What are you working on?"

"French. Aren't two languages enough?" I actually

liked Madam Hummel, even though French was far from my favorite class. She was the kind of person who I felt wouldn't laugh if she caught the boys slapping Kaylee's butt. I'd been thinking about that: Rachel, saying nobody cared. There were a few teachers who I thought would. Like Ms. O'Dell. She had a poster on her wall of Malala Yousafzai with a quote that said "I raise up my voice, not so I can shout, but so that those without a voice can be heard." For homework this week I had to make a recording about a flawed world figure, and she'd given the example of Woodrow Wilson, who was president when women got the right to vote but was actually super sexist. Our science teacher would care, too—Dr. Abioye, with his calm voice and goofy ties. He'd helped me find a couple of documentaries to watch for my penguin project. He didn't put up with any crap.

"If they offered Polish, I'd let you take it," she said. "Easy A. Hey, this one's for Nik. Nikola!" My sister got a lot of mail—mostly flyers from colleges. I'm not sure how every university within two hundred miles knew that she was sixteen, but they must have their ways, because she got new brochures in the mail every single week. This letter looked different, though. It was a plain white envelope with our address written in messy handwriting.

My sister came down the stairs, hair falling out of her bun. "Whoa. What's with the art project?"

"I'm *volunteering*," Mom said. "It's what good mothers *do* at public school, apparently."

"You're a whole new woman," she said.

"Well, *you've* got mail," Mom reported. "Ha. Like the AOL guy."

"Your age is showing, old lady," I said. "The hip kids text now."

"That's such a good movie, though," Nik said, ripping open the envelope. She pulled out some loose-leaf papers. A *lot* of them.

"Whoa. What's that?" Mom asked.

Nik started to read it, and her shoulders dropped. Her mouth did, too, a little bit. It was like she forgot we were watching her. I was surprised she didn't take it into her room to read it, but I think once she realized what it was, she wanted her people around her. You don't want to open a letter like that by yourself, the same way Nik had told me you don't want to go on strange websites that are written on scraps of paper and shoved in your locker.

"Nik. You look like someone sent you a *death threat*. What is it?" Mom reached for the papers, but she snatched them away.

"It's . . . it's nothing," she said. "Just a letter."

"A *letter*? I thought the hip kids texted. Who sent you a letter? You're upset." That was Mom: to the point. No sense in tiptoeing around the truth. Mom didn't tiptoe, metaphorically or in real life. You always knew where she was in the house.

"I'm . . . This guy. The one I told you about. Bronson. He—"

"The one who won't leave you alone?" Mom asked. "Let me see that. No, stop—I mean it." Nik handed the letter to Mom, who started to read it.

"What's it say?" I asked.

Mom's mouth did the same thing Nik's had, and my sister just stared out the window into the dark backyard. Jesse, that sweet dog, recognized she needed some love. He trotted right over and sat by her feet.

"I want to read it," I said.

"Nik," Mom said, ignoring me. "This isn't good. This is *bizarre*. What, eight pages of this? Anna, go do your homework in your room. Your sister and I need to have a private conversation."

"I want to know, too," I said. I sounded like a whiny little sister, even to my own ears.

"Anna Maria, do I sound like I'm debating this right now? Go."

I dragged my school stuff up to my room, but

it's not like I couldn't hear most of what they were saying anyway. *Scary* and *be firm* and *our address* from Mom. *Embarrassing* and *don't know* and *I tried* from Nik.

They talked for a long, long time, even after Dad got home and I heard him join them at the table. I got all ready for bed and crawled in, feeling a little ticked off, to be honest. But more than that, feeling a little nervous. That my tough, brave sister could be sent creepy letters by boys she knew—it just didn't seem right. But then again, wasn't Rachel Riley tough and brave? Tough and brave doesn't necessarily equal *protection*.

Like always, I couldn't sleep. I *especially* couldn't sleep once I started thinking about how I couldn't sleep. Even more so once all of the lights went off in the house. I hated being the last one awake. But there was no doubt about it—I was.

I was dreading the stupid winter dance that weekend, which wasn't helping my insomnia. It was all anyone at school could talk about. Bee had spent all of French class whispering to me about this new dress her mom had ordered her from a fancy boutique in London. I'd overheard Kaylee in the lunch line talking about how she planned to do her hair. And Mom had asked me a bunch of times if I wanted to go shopping before giving up and presenting me with three options she found on Pinterest. I'd picked a simple blue dress with some lace around the bottom, because it reminded me of snowflakes, and it was supposed to be the Winter Ball. But I just couldn't get excited about standing around a sweaty gym with a bunch of boys who grabbed girls in weird ways. It creeped me out.

I must have fallen asleep eventually, because at 3:00 a.m., I jolted awake. I sat straight up, because a thought had shoved its way into my brain, even in my weird half-asleep state.

Rachel Riley wasn't planning to go to our high school next year. She was going to Moorland, if everything worked out for her. And not to get away from mean kids—according to Cody, she'd always wanted to go there, for music. Everyone assumed she'd get in. That meant she *knew*, when she burned down the Kincaid Farms Event Barn, that she wasn't likely going to have to put up with kids being mad at her for long.

And what had she said? That it didn't matter what you did. Nothing was going to make them stop. So why would she have written a note to Blake, saying she was going to tell on him? Answer: she wouldn't.

One other thing, too, that had been gnawing at

me. *How* had Rachel gotten into the barn? It had a huge, heavy door. I'd seen it, at Harvest Fest *and* the day I tried to find Sierra. Had she broken a window and climbed in? But Rachel was short—one of the shortest girls in the eighth grade. Small, too. She'd need help—someone to lift her, or something. Could she have started the fire from the outside? But then how could it have possibly been an accident? But if she *did* have help, wouldn't everybody know about it?

You can have evidence, or you can have a gut feeling. Sometimes both. This was my gut, pure and simple: Rachel Riley was covering for someone. Someone else was there the night of June 4, and only Rachel Riley knew who.

14

NOVEMBER 21

To: LIST: Parents of East Eighth Graders

From: Principal Lila Howe <lhowe@east.middle.edu>

Subj: Winter Ball fiasco

Parents of East Eighth Graders,

I am writing to officially apologize for the debacle that occurred
at our eighth-grade Winter Ball. I assume you have heard bits
and pieces of what transpired from your eighth-grade student.
It saddens me deeply that both dances we've planned for this
particular class of kids have ended in mayhem, destruction,
and complete and utter disaster.

Regrettably, we had a lack of parental volunteers for the
event itself, which may have led to the spiraling of unfortunate

events. Instead of relying on the local grapevine to tell you the full and complete story, I've launched my own investigation and cobbled together a timeline of events so that you have as clear of a picture as possible.

It's important to ensure we have all of the facts straight, so I am writing to you today as both princi-PAL and principal fact finder.

7:00: Students were dropped off at the East Middle School gymnasium for the Winter Ball. They were greeted by our dance cochairs, Lana McLeen and Maja Hunt. Attendance was soon at around seventy-five students, or approximately three-quarters of our eighth-grade class.

7:30: A small commotion broke out between two of our female students. This was handled quickly and discreetly by a parent volunteer.

8:00: One of the girls, a student who has been the victim of some unfortunate childish bullying this year, asked the DJ if she could make a quick announcement. DJ Funkee-Funk, who was *not* on East Middle School's approved contractor list (the cochairs of the dance have been reprimanded for hiring him without district approval), agreed to hand over the microphone. 8:02: The female student began speaking into the microphone about an allegation of sexual harassment. Let me be clear:

East Middle School takes sexual harassment *extremely* seriously. That being said, naming specific boys and girls involved in this alleged harassment over a microphone at a school dance is not the proper channel to air a grievance.

8:05: One of the accused boys angrily led a chant with a word that is not appropriate for a school environment, directed at this female student.

8:07: A separate female student secured a glass bowl of punch and proceeded to pour it over the boy in question.

8:08: The boy in question tripped on the power cord that was being used for the elaborate lights display.

8:09: The gymnasium was pitched into darkness, where additional punch was thrown, chairs were tripped over, and students were injured.

8:15: DJ Funkee-Funk—*who, again, was not on East Middle School's approved contractor list*—said an expletive into his microphone and accused our East Knights of being, and I quote, "absolute animals."

8:17: Eleanor McIlhenry, our trusted custodian, was able to get the lights back on.

8:20: I announced over the speakers that the remainder of the dance was canceled and that students were to wait in the hallway for their parents to pick them up. Parents and guardians were immediately notified via our emergency text system.

It is *most* unfortunate that the bad decisions of a select few students are to blame for the cancellation of the eighth-grade Winter Ball. But we've learned a few valuable lessons from this experience that we will utilize going forward.

All dance cochairs are to be thoroughly vetted by me, personally.

Any student who resorts to any type of violence, including, but not limited to, dousing classmates in beverages, will automatically be banned from school-sponsored activities for the rest of the year.

In order to prevent blackouts, we will no longer use any light displays that require additional power cords. This will prevent any unintended chaos.

Please let me know if you have any further questions or concerns about your child's participation in the Winter Ball. Dr. Fayen, our guidance counselor, is also available to chat with your children at any time regarding any feelings of stress or frustration they may be feeling as a result of the event.

I would also like to formally apologize that the frosting on the cookies *did* include artificial food coloring.

And let's not forget to remind our children every day as they head off to school—peace begins with us!

Regards,
Lila Howe
Principal
East Middle School

NOVEMBER 22

To: Maja Hunt <mhunt@wisc.edu>

From: Lana McLeen <lana@lanamcleen.com>

Subj: FWD: Winter Ball fiasco

Maja,

Can you BELIEVE this garbage? After all I've done for that school—did Lila just "forget" that I've helped plan every event since the back-to-school barbecue when Cody was a sixth grader?! The audacity of that woman to imply that *you and I* are at fault for the reckless behavior of these children! Peace begins with us, *my hat*!!!

Xo

Lana McLeen

Wedding Queen

www.lanamcleen.com

Reach out about YOUR event TODAY!

PS: Maybe if the old miser had given us a larger DJ budget than two hundred dollars, I could have found someone better than my assistant's nephew to play music!

NOVEMBER 22

To: Lana McLeen <lana@lanamcleen.com>

From: Maja Hunt <mhunt@wisc.edu>

Subj: Re: FWD: Winter Ball fiasco

Lana,

In all honesty, if this gets me out of parental volunteering for the rest of the year, I'm glad. Best of luck.

Sincerely,

Maja Hunt, Attorney-at-Law

Professor

University of Wisconsin–Madison

NOVEMBER 22

Bee:
So . . . grounded?

Anna:
They're "still deciding."
My parents aren't big
grounders . . . Mom said
it sounded like Blake
deserved it

Bee:
You're lucky. I'd be dead lol. I can't
believe you were even able to pick up
that punch bowl. It looked heavy!

Anna:
um, *I* can't believe
Rachel told the boys she
was going to dox every
single one of them on
Instagram next time she
saw someone's bra get
snapped

Bee:
lol. I can. That's so Rachel . . . she's
always making a huge deal out of stuff

Anna:
Yeah but don't you think
it is kind of a huge deal?
I saw Blake snap yours
right when we got there.

Bee:
I don't care. I can stand up for MYSELF.
No I don't like it but like I don't want to
be seen as one of those super dramatic
girls you know? It's best just to act like
it doesn't bother you or they make you
a target. Besides I can't believe Rachel
even came. Nobody likes her

Anna:
I do

Bee:
. . . k

Anna:
What's that supposed to mean?

Bee:
I mean we all USED to like her! She's
fun and nice and whatever. She was
maybe even gonna get the 🌹 award last
year before she messed everything up

Anna:
Wait, she was?? Isn't that
the award for being the
kindest student?

Bee:
Forget I said anything

Anna:
Who got it instead?

Bee:
Nobody. The whole thing was canceled
remember? I gotta go to bed. See you
tmr in French

NOVEMBER 22

Cody:
RU in trouble at all?

:

No. My mom was proud. Haha.

Cody:
I couldn't believe you came.

:

I had to do something. AGAIN.

Cody:
I know you hate me and everything,
but I was thinking about those turkeys
yesterday, on Thanksgiving. Just like
you said. And you know what else I
remembered?

:
?

Cody:
How when our families would go camping together, we'd always wait for the trees to go gold as the sun went down. For that one minute, when they'd kind of look like magic. We called them magic trees. I saw them yesterday, when the sun went down.

Cody:
I wish we were still friends.

🌲:

I wish you'd make them stop.

🌲:

But I remember the magic trees, too.

"A BOWL OF PUNCH, ANNA? I MEAN, COME ON," DAD said. It was Thanksgiving. Piles of mashed potatoes, that pool of gravy—a holiday dedicated to eating? I could get behind that. Most kids had cousins and grandparents and neighbors all packed around their table, but Dad's parents had died before I was born, and he was an only child. Mom's mom and sister were still back in Poland—Babcia and Ciocia Elza. Thanksgiving for us was always tiny and cozy.

But, of course, our dinner had turned into our one millionth rehashing of the Winter Ball. Nik couldn't get enough of it.

"I didn't know what to do! You heard them, Mom. *Rachel Riley is a*—"

"Stop." She held up her hand. "That word is not to be spoken under my roof. I told your dad, you shouldn't be grounded. You should be given a medal. Lila is never going to make me volunteer for anything ever again. I'll probably be banned from events from now on."

"Maja," Dad said, "she used *violence* . . ."

"Jamie," Mom retorted, "she threw some punch. That kid laughed. He didn't even care. He seemed like a real punk."

"Blake Wyatt," I said.

"*Blake Wyatt*, Blake Wyatt?" Nik asked me, eyebrow raised. I nodded.

"Sister secrets. No fair. You don't have a *crush* on that goon, do you, Anna?" Mom asked, salting her turkey.

"Not even a little," I said flatly.

"Good. Because I must say, he didn't exactly give off Prince Charming vibes," Mom said.

Dad shook his head. "Especially if what Rachel said was true. That the boys are running around snapping the girls' . . ."

"Bras, Dad. You can say it," said Nik. For a guy who lived with three girls, the words "bra" or "tampon" could still make Dad clam up.

"Nobody's ever done that to you, have they, Anna?" Mom asked. "I mean, is what she said *true*?"

"Not to me," I said, ignoring the second part of her question. Not like there'd be anything to snap. My bras were the kind you wear just to make yourself feel better about being thirteen.

"Hey, you want me to save all of those cans?" Dad

asked. "For your Social Issues project? Instead of tossing them in the recycling bin?"

"Oh yeah. Thanks."

"How's that coming, Anna Maria?" Mom asked me, an eyebrow raised.

"Terrific," I lied. Well . . . it was terrific in my head. Terrifically easy. Terrifically simple. Terrifically unstarted. But really, how long could it take to glue a bunch of garbage to a sheet of paper? It'd be fine.

"You should have done something about penguins. Then you could double-dip your research," Nik pointed out. "Gender stereotypes! Don't the dads stay with the eggs while the moms go hunting?"

"We're a penguin family," Mom joked, leaning over and giving Dad a kiss on the cheek. "Minus the feathers."

That afternoon, Nik and Dad scrubbed the dishes while Mom and I went on a turkey-burning walk with the dogs.

"Moving your legs should be a requirement after eating that much pumpkin pie. It's all just *sitting there*," Mom said. She was right. Mom wasn't the kind of parent who bought weird fake health food or talked about trans fats, thank God, but she *was* the kind of parent who liked to get outside and move. Kix was feeling extra chatty, barking at every squirrel he saw and howling at the other dogs in the neighborhood to say hello. Jesse kept glancing back at us as if to say *Do you see what I have to put up with?*

"Dad should have been a chef, not a lawyer," I said.

She smiled. "That's nice. You're a nice kid, you know that?"

"Did you just compliment me?" I said. It must have come out kind of harsh, because Mom gave me a look.

"I believe I offered you a medal, like, twenty minutes ago," she said.

I shrugged. "I guess. I just feel like since we moved here it's been . . . *Are you making friends? Are you fitting in? Are you being nice?* Like it's all up to me to make sure I'm some kind of cool social butterfly instead of . . . Anna."

Mom stopped walking and looked at me carefully. I stopped, too.

"I'm sorry I'm not making all these new friends, like Nik. And I'm sorry I'd rather read a book than talk to a bunch of my kids at school. I wish I were more like you. All . . ."

"All what?" she asked, cocking her head to the side.

"All *confident* and stuff," I said. "Like I could talk to anyone."

"Anna," she said slowly, "all I've ever wanted is for you to be yourself."

"But maybe I don't even know what that means!" I burst out. "I'm not all *tough*, like you and Nik. I'm just . . ."

"Anna. If I made you feel like you were supposed to be more like me, I'm sorry," she said softly. "I just . . . I always *had* to be so tough, you know? Immigrant speaking here. We had *nothing* growing up, and I mean nothing. I came to college and barely spoke English. Law school, too. I always had to be so . . . strong. It's hard to go through life as a girl. I mean, it's hard to go through life as *anyone*. Especially eighth grade. But I never, ever wanted you to feel like you had to be someone you're not."

"Sometimes, I just feel like . . . I don't know. I'm too much. Too weird, or something. Too . . . bookworm-y." I said. "Like it'd be easier if I was just one of those people who didn't care about anything important. But I do."

Mom nodded. "I know what you mean. But don't be *afraid* of caring, either. We need people who care."

"Even if punch-throwing is part of the caring?"

Mom laughed. "I get it. You wanted to do something immediate. But there are other ways. Better ways."

"Turn the other cheek," I said in my solemn Father Andrew voice.

"Yes and no. Forgiveness, sure—that's important. But so is justice. I'm talking about a justice that involves *words*, and *love*, and *accountability*. All the good stuff. None of the violent beverage-tossing."

We walked the rest of the way home in silence, but as we turned onto our street, Mom stopped, grabbed my shoulder.

"Listen, Anna Maria. I get worried, that you care so much that you make yourself so anxious. I worry things will be hard for you. But I don't want to make you scared of being *you*. You don't take up too much space. It's other people's smallness, not your largeness, that needs work. Okay?"

I nodded.

"And . . . you'd tell me if any of the boys at school did something that made you uncomfortable, right?"

I nodded again, but this time with less certainty.

"Now, come on," she said turning toward home. "Let's see if we can stuff one more piece of pie in our stomachs."

≥ **15** ≤

NOVEMBER 27

To: Katarzyna Kowalski <babciakat@gmail.com>
From: Anna Hunt <ahunt@east.middle.edu>
Subj: Truth + penguins, penguins + truth

Babcia,

What you said made a lot of sense. You're right: it's hard to
tell the truth when you feel like you're the only one. When
you write about growing up in communism, and how scary it
was to say things the government didn't agree with . . . that's
intense. Remember when we went to the solidarity museum

in Gdańsk? You showed me those pictures of the tanks rolling down the streets. You talked about seeing them in your little neighborhood, and how your mom cried.

I wish I could say that it made me feel closer to you. But the truth is, I feel like it makes my problems feel small. Nobody's going to throw me in jail for telling on a boy. Mom told me that Dziadek once got beaten up by the police for being outside after curfew. *That's* real trouble, isn't it?

But does it make *my* troubles any less? Or Rachel Riley's troubles?

And that question—who do you *trust*? That's still there, too. You don't *know* who to trust, is the problem. Especially when your trust has been broken already. Trust is kind of a fragile thing. Once it gets cracked, it's hard to put it back together.

There are some people I trust no matter what, but it's a small circle. You. Mom and Dad. Nik. My *family* . . . I know they'd never hurt me, but even then, I don't know who I can tell things to, always.

I love, love, love (and trust, trust, trust) you.

Penguin fun fact of the day: penguins huddle together not just for warmth, but to protect themselves from predators. There's strength in numbers. Those little birds are smart.

Love,
Anna

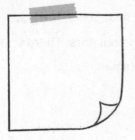

NOVEMBER 28

Principal Howe,

As part of my punishment for the Winter Ball disturbance, I was told to write an apology letter to you.

I was going to just say sorry. I really was. I try to be a nice person. Saying "sorry" is such an easy thing to do, and when you say it, it's kind of like an end to an argument. If you don't want someone to be mad at you anymore, you just say "sorry." It's a get-out-of-jail-free card.

But what if you aren't sorry? Then your sorry is a lie. That's not doing the right thing.

I wish I could just say "sorry." Honestly—I really do. If I could say sorry for what I did at the winter dance, I wouldn't be in trouble anymore. If I could say sorry for burning down the barn last year, everyone would forgive me. If I could say sorry for making a commotion about something wrong, everything would be smoother and easier.

But smoother and easier doesn't always mean better. It may seem like the more peaceful thing. But being silent about something bad—that's not peaceful. That's just going along.

So I'm not sorry.

In fact, the more I think about it, the less sorry I am.

Sincerely,
Rachel M. Riley

NOVEMBER 29

To: Kristy Riley <kristy.riley@rileygraphics.com>
From: Principal Lila Howe <lhowe@east.middle.edu>
Subj: Rachel's apology

Kristy and Todd,

Please see Rachel's note, scanned and attached below. At this point, I have no other choice but to ban Rachel from any school-sponsored activities for the rest of the year. She will also need to report to a three-day in-school suspension.

You inquired as to whether the accusations she made at the Winter Ball will be looked into. The brief answer is yes, but I can't give any further details at this time since our process is still ongoing. Furthermore, the boy responsible for starting the chant has also been asked to draft an apology email, which he did immediately. Therefore, he will not be given an in-school suspension.

I know Rachel is a wonderful student who has applied for Moorland Academy of the Arts. I'd hate to see her behavior continue to plummet as this year continues. Contacting Moorland to revoke my letter of recommendation would be a huge blow to her, particularly given her misdemeanor last spring. Please ensure she's focused on her studies, not further disruptions.

Sincerely,
Lila Howe

NOVEMBER 29

To: LIST: Staff of East Middle School

From: Lila Howe <lhowe@east.middle.edu>

Subj: You can do it!

Staff members,

I know many of you either witnessed or heard about the debacle at the eighth-grade winter dance. I would like to remind you all of East Middle School's sexual harassment policy, attached here as a PDF. Anyone seen creating a hostile educational environment should be brought to my office immediately.

I know this group of students has seemed exceptionally difficult this year. Rest assured, we're almost to winter break— hang in there.

Best,

Lila Howe

AFTER THANKSGIVING BREAK, WALKING THROUGH THE hall felt like walking through mud. Those few weeks between Thanksgiving and Christmas, teachers don't really want to start anything, so it's a lot of movies or "silent work time," and "silent work time" basically just meant "time to talk to your friends." Blake and his crew obviously hated me now, but Jordan and Kaylee were acting mad at me, too. Bee was out sick—she had strep, she'd texted me, and could I please send her which chapters to read for French? So for most of the day, I was just completely by myself. I felt like Rachel Riley, to be honest. Apparently, after throwing that punch on Blake, I was on her social level. AKA: the ground floor. Or underground.

At lunch, I sat in my usual all-alone spot. The same table as Rachel. I wondered what would have happened if I'd just tried to be her friend this year instead of doing the whole podcast project. Maybe neither of us would be alone at lunch. Instead, we both were.

She pulled out a book, gave me a nod, and started eating her lunch. She hadn't been in algebra, the only class I had with her, and I heard she'd been given an in-school suspension. All I'd had to do was write an apology email to Principal Howe. I wanted to ask her about the dance—how she'd gotten the courage to do what she did. Maybe she'd even agree to talk to me for the podcast again. But just as I opened my mouth to ask her, the loudspeaker came on.

Attention, East Knight eighth graders, a voice said over the lunchroom intercom. *Today is December first, and we have some birthdays to celebrate. Please put your hands together for . . . Tavonna Jackson-Vacek!* Claps, hoots, hollers—mostly from the table where the soccer kids sat. *Mallory Ramsey!* More cheers, this time from the artsy group that gave each other Sharpie tattoos during outside time. *And Cody McLeen.* Hollers from the popular table. Blake stood on his seat and made some weird, warrior *whoo-whoo-whoo* sound, which cracked everyone up. Of course he had to make everything about himself.

And then—I realized something.

Something *big*.

December 1. 12/01.

BilboBaggins1201.

A thousand years ago, in the library: a Gandalf

Lord of the Rings sweatshirt. *I like to read*, he'd snapped at Lee's Dairy Emporium.

And *then* . . . I choked on my sandwich.

I've never choked on anything before. I mean, things have gone down the wrong pipe, but this was way worse than that. I felt like I couldn't breathe. I started coughing as hard as I could, grabbing my water bottle and chugging, but that only made it worse. I was gasping for air, and I heard Jordan yell, "Anna! Anna's choking!" Before I knew it, someone's arms were around me—Ms. Anyanwu, the Computer Literacy teacher, who was the cafeteria aide that day. She kind of punched her fists up into my stomach, and—oh, *gross*—the piece of sandwich launched back out of my mouth and onto the table.

The entire cafeteria probably didn't burst into an *eww*, but that's how it felt. I didn't even say thank you to Ms. Anyanwu. I just grabbed my backpack, ditching the rest of my lunch on the table, and took off for my locker. I had to text Nik—now.

My locker was right down the hall from the cafeteria. My hands were shaking as I opened the lock.

"Hey. *No phones*, Miss Hunt." I turned around, expecting to see a teacher, but it was Trevor Frey, doing a fake teacher voice. He was coming out of the boys' bathroom.

I rolled my eyes and ignored him. "I have to send a text."

"Phones aren't allowed out on school property," he said in his fake teacher voice. "Don't make me give you a *detention!*"

"Goodbye, Trevor," I said pointedly.

And that's when it happened. He leaned over, pinched the back of my T-shirt, and—snap.

Ow. I have to admit, I hadn't really thought this entire time about how much it *hurt* to have your strap snapped. I'd thought of the embarrassment level, sure, but the adjuster clip slapping against my shoulder—I hadn't realized how much that would sting.

"You don't need to have such an attitude. I was *joking,*" he said. He *laughed.*

"Please don't do that again," I said. I tried to sound strong, but my voice was wavering. Polite yet clear. I imagined Nik: tall, strong Nik. But then again, I imagined Bronson Webb, and that long letter. A written-down bra-strap snap. *Taking,* just sent through the mail instead.

"Dude, you're one of those crazy chicks. I forgot. You and Rachel," he said. "Don't worry. You're only, like, two points." And then he went off down the hallway. Not in any kind of hurry, like he was worried about getting in trouble. Not like he had anywhere to *be*. Just meandering. Like he had all the time in the world, all the freedom in the world.

Because he did. At least, that's how it felt.

I wish I could say that I ran after him, yelled at him in his face. Or turned around and told Ms. Anyanwu what had happened. At the bare minimum, that I texted my sister and told her about it. But I didn't. Instead, I just heard his voice: *You're only, like, two points*. I don't know why that hurt almost as much as the bra-strap snap, but it did.

So here's the truth of what I did: strong girl, tough girl, my mother's daughter. I went into the bathroom and cried.

>16<

DECEMBER 2

Anna: This is WHAT HAPPENED TO RACHEL RILEY?: AN INVESTIGATION BY ANNA HUNT. *I'm speaking with Cody McLeen.*

Cody: Hi.

Anna: What made you change your mind and decide to talk to me?

Cody: I mean, you already know I made the site. I figure you're going to tell on me anyway. I might as well get to tell my side of the story.

Anna: When I asked you if you were BilboBaggins1201, what made you cop to it?

<pause>

Anna: I said, when I—

Cody: I heard you. I'm just thinking.

Cody: You ever have something on your mind that takes up so much space you just need to say it to get it out?

Anna: Yeah. I do.

Cody: It was like that. I'm tired of having secrets. I'm tired of—all of this. Tired of pretending I didn't do . . . this bad thing. That I did.

Anna: Making the website?

Cody: Making the website. Letting things get out of hand.

Anna: So . . . how'd the game even get started? Maybe we should begin there.

Cody: I guess you'd have to go back to last year. February, maybe. It was cold. Freezing, man . . . My cousins live in California, and whenever they post pictures in the winter I get annoyed. It was, like, zero degrees for a week. We all took outside time in the library. And we'd been talking about the girls. Yeah, maybe not in a super-nice way . . . but just talking about them. Who was hot. Who we wanted to . . . you know, kiss and stuff. This sounds stupid.

Anna: Kind of.

Cody: Whatever. That's what guys talk about, right? I don't know why we don't have anything better to talk about. But is it so bad to notice? What girls look like?

So we started ranking them. Who we thought had the nicest butt. Okay, now this sounds really stupid. But everyone agreed Jordan was the hottest girl in seventh grade. And then Blake dared Carlos.

Anna: What'd he dare him?

Cody: To slap her on the butt.

Anna: Did he?

Cody: Yeah. He did. But Carlos said if he did it, if he slapped Jordan on the butt, Blake had to slap Chelsea.

Anna: So that's how it started.

Cody: And it was just, like, a snowball or something. I didn't do the slapping, because every time I thought about it—this is so dumb. But I just thought of my mom, and what she would say. Whenever she finds out about an actor or someone who did something weird to a woman, she always gets so down. Presidents, you know?

Anna: Yeah.

Cody: It's like, that's what boys do. They have locker-room talk. That's what I heard a guy say on the news. But I don't know if we've ever stopped to be like, Maybe that shouldn't be locker-room talk. *And we weren't in a locker room! Anyway. I didn't do the slapping, I swear, but I didn't stop it, either. And we were keeping points on Blake's phone. But then . . .*

Anna: What happened?

Cody: They started kind of messing with me. Asking why I was so chicken, maybe I was gay, maybe—just being jerks.

Anna: You do realize your friends sound like people I wouldn't want to be around for ten seconds, right?

Cody: Yeah. I don't really like being around them, either, most of the time. But sometimes they're cool. Sometimes. You know, people aren't just . . . one thing. There's more to them than butt-slapping and points and stuff.

Anna: It's hard to see it when they act the way they're acting.

Cody: I get that. Yeah. So anyway, they were just being so obnoxious. I was annoyed. And we'd just learned how to make really basic sites in Computer Lit, and I was pretty into it. I made one for our family photos, and my mom loved it. So one day, I just . . . got bored and made the site. I wanted to get them off my back. It only took a couple hours. The guys loved it. And it made everything easy to track. I didn't even mean for the girls to find out about it. But—I mean, you know how this stuff is. People talk. They did find out, somehow. And suddenly everyone was checking it every day.

Anna: How do you think it made the girls feel?

Cody: Are you trying to make me feel like I'm on trial?

Anna: No. I'm trying to make you think about someone other than yourself.

Cody: They hated it. But they didn't know I made the website.

Anna: So why'd you wipe it?

Cody: After what happened at the barn, and then Rachel getting blamed for it, and everyone thinking she wrote that note to Blake . . . it was just time to be done. Things were getting out of control. I was going to get in serious trouble, you know? We all were. The girls acted like they thought it was funny, too, but they didn't. Rachel especially—I mean, we were really good friends. The guys always gave me crap about dating her or being into her, but I swear, I really wasn't. We'd just been friends since we were little kids. She was like my sister. And she hated that website. She hated the game. The guys were worst to her and Jordan.

Anna: How come?

Cody: Jordan because she's pretty and funny and laughed about it. She just kind of goes along with whatever. She's chill. Rachel because . . . well, she's pretty, too, but it kind of seemed to get a rise out of her. That was fun for some of the guys. Ticking her off.

Anna: So why did the game come back this year?

Cody: I don't know. I don't! I didn't start this whole stupid thing, okay? Chelsea had that bright bra on; she obviously wanted someone to see it—

Anna: That's not how that works. She forgot—you know what, never mind. I don't have to explain her underwear choices to you.

Cody: I know that. I'm not a jerk, okay? I know that.

Anna: You know that . . . but you cheered it on anyway. What good is the knowing if you're not going to use it to make choices that don't suck?

Cody: I'm not Carlos. Maybe I cheered, but I didn't start it. But these things just get started and keep going, and now . . . Blake wants me to turn the website back on. But I won't. So he's keeping track on his phone. There's no prize or anything this time. It's just a game.

Anna: What about Rachel?

Cody: What about her?

Anna: Why did you stop being friends? Were you mad at her, too?

Cody: No. Rachel was mad at me. She was mad that I didn't do enough to—to make them stop. Last year, and now this year, too. She thinks I have power I don't have.

Anna: Did you? Ever ask them to stop, I mean?

Cody: I started to push back a little bit, yeah, but

it was tough. I know what you're thinking. Poor Cody, boo-hoo, doesn't know how to stand up for himself. *But it's hard when everyone around you is laughing about something. You try getting through middle school with no friends. Do you have any idea what that feels like?*

Anna: Yes. And I think Rachel Riley does, too.

DECEMBER 2

Anna: Sorry—I have one final question I forgot to ask. Thanks for meeting back up.

Cody: What's up?

Anna: You said, "Rachel getting blamed for burning down the barn."

Cody: Yeah?

Anna: You didn't say, "Rachel burning down the barn." But she was caught there. Do you think she's innocent?

Anna: Cody?

Cody: I think people make choices. I think I chose to be a bad friend. I think Rachel chose to be a good one. That's all I'm going to say about it.

POLICE REPORT

FILED: JUNE 6, 2021
ACCESSED DECEMBER 3

FILING OFFICER: JOSEPH A. GILMORE

At approximately 12:14 a.m. on June 5, the Madison Fire Department responded to a call reporting smoke coming from the direction of Kincaid Farms. A fire truck with six fire personnel reported to the scene. Three additional officers arrived. At the scene, a minor was apprehended, holding a lighter.

The fire was quickly put out, but the damage to the barn was substantial. No humans or animals were inside the barn at the time of the fire. The estimated property damage was in the hundreds of thousands.

When brought in for questioning, the minor admitted to trespassing with the intention of swapping out the names of award winners for a seventh-grade awards ceremony, which was to be held at the barn the following day. While she was in the process of swapping the cards, a lantern she had been using for light was knocked over, and a fire quickly started.

The minor insisted she was alone on the premises. Her bicycle, a pink Schwinn, was parked just outside of the barn. However, clear tire tracks in the mud show that another bicycle had been present at the scene of the crime. The minor denies any accomplices and insists she does not know who the other bicycle tracks belong to. The minor was also found with a key on her person. She reports stealing the key from her next-door neighbor, a local wedding planner who would have had easy access to the venue.

Unfortunately, Kincaid Farms did not have adequate security equipment, so all the Madison Police Department has for evidence is the testimony of the minor.

═══════════════════════════════════════

DECEMBER 6

Bee:
Hey . . . I saw what happened after
math. U ok?

Anna:
I thought you thought the
game wasn't a big deal.

Bee:
idk you looked upset

Anna:
I was. But I'm fine.

"YOU NEED TO SEE THIS," SAID NIK, THE SECOND she walked in the door.

"See what?" I asked. I was tired. Tired of Rachel Riley and of Cody McLeen. Tired of feeling like there was destruction around every corner. Tired of looking over the police report someone had shoved into my locker. Tired of wondering who those other bike tracks belonged to. Tired of not sleeping.

Nik was throwing a lot of energy into the Rachel Riley project. She'd shown me emails from Mom's laptop—emails from Principal Howe saying what had happened at the Winter Ball. She'd even found a way into Principal Howe's email. *Couldn't you go to jail for that?* I asked, and she just rolled her eyes, and showed me how Principal Howe had had to email Rachel's mom about Harvest Fest. She seemed more focused on the project than she'd ever been on code. She seemed *fired up*, to be honest. A mission can do that to people.

"I found something on the website today." She sat down next to me on the couch and pulled out her laptop. Dad was chopping onions in the kitchen, and Mom was upstairs taking a shower. Italian music was playing, and the smell of spaghetti sauce was in the air. Kix and Jesse were even happy with each other, curled up on an afghan in front of the fireplace. I felt like I was in a little nest of coziness. I didn't want to stop and think about slapping butts or snapping bra straps. I was in the middle of a book about dragons and quests and faraway things. But Nik opened her laptop and clicked a few keystrokes.

"I didn't think to really go through the website, because, duh, all it is is a scorecard. But I was clicking around on it today, taking some screenshots—"

"Why?" I asked.

She shrugged. "In case you decide to do something with it. Something other than your school project." That's what Nik thought I had to do: do something with it. I knew where she was coming from.

But today, after math, it had happened again. I was at my locker, just getting out my science textbook, and there it was—a hand on my back, a *snap*. I even had a sweatshirt on—he'd practically had to *dig*. I turned around, pissed, but Trevor was already jogging down the hall. He looked over his shoulder and laughed. Not even in a mean way, but like he genuinely thought *I* was going to laugh, too.

I didn't.

I didn't laugh. I didn't tell him to stop. And I didn't tell a teacher. Partly because of what Rachel had said—not all teachers could be trusted, could they? Partly because I just couldn't picture opening my mouth to say the words. And partly because if I did . . .

Well, what if what happened to Rachel happened to me?

What if *I* was their new favorite target?

What if *I* was the one who couldn't even walk down the halls without getting harassed, which suddenly didn't feel like a big, ugly word . . . but an accurate one?

"Okay, so look," Nik said. "I totally missed this when we first looked at the site, but after clicking around the last version of it before it got wiped, I found this. It was captured the first week of May." She scrolled to the bottom of what seemed like a blank page and stopped when she came to a paragraph in thick, bold text:

GRAND PRIZE: Whoever has the highest amount of points by the day of Spring Fling will kiss Jordan Russell after the awards ceremony.

"Anna. That's sick," said Nik. *"Sick."*

I stared at the computer screen. "That's what Cody said today. There's not a prize or anything this time. I didn't even realize . . . there was one before."

"What were they gonna do, hold her down?" Nik shivered.

"She said it was just a stupid game," I said. "I wonder if she knew this was coming."

"I mean, it was a public website, and they all knew about it, right? She had to. Why do you think they picked her?"

I shrugged. "She's pretty. Besides, she's not the kind of girl who's going to say anything. She would have let it happen, probably, without getting that mad. She's not like Rachel."

"Or you," said Nik.

Or me? Yeah, right.

I wished. I wished like anything I were like that, but instead, I felt my eyes getting wet. Oh, crap—I am *not* a crier. Honestly. I'm just not that kind of girl. And this was twice in a week. But before I knew it, there I was, crying.

"Anna—I didn't mean to . . . What's wrong? I thought you'd be excited. Doesn't this help with your project?"

Trevor, that bra strap—twice. And who was I?

Not Rachel Riley. Not someone who stood up for herself. I thought I was Tris and Katniss and Éowyn and Hermione, all of these brave girls who could fight giants and win battles. But I wasn't. Not even a little bit. Not even at all.

I told my sister and my mom. Of course I did. I was done with the keeping secrets. Mothers and sisters and grandmothers: these are the people we have in our corner, the people that make being a girl bearable. Dad, maybe he would have gotten it, but Mom sent him on some errands, and we sat at the kitchen table with big cups of hot chocolate. Three women, strong and tough and scared and tired. I told about the podcast, and I told about the bra straps, and I told about Trevor Frey. I talked until my throat was sore.

"You have to say what you mean, and mean what you say," Mom said. "You're in charge of you. You can't help what Jordan, or Bee, or any of the other girls do."

"Jordan didn't want to hurt their feelings, I think," I said. "She didn't want to seem dramatic . . . she's just—*nice*."

Mom shook her head. "Other People's Feelings is too heavy of a weight to carry."

"'Nice' can be another word for 'scared,'" Nik said.

"We're *supposed* to care about other people's

feelings." It was true. Aren't we taught that in kindergarten? The golden rule. Using nice words. Those were the most important things. *Manners.*

"We're supposed to be honest, and we're supposed to be kind. Honesty plus kindness equals your responsibility," said Mom. "How *other* people respond? *Their* emotions? *Their* opinion of you? Not your job."

"Honest," I said. "Nik's room smells like something died in there."

Nik leaned forward and flicked me on the temple. "I haven't done laundry in, like, a week and a half. I've been *busy.* Sleep in your own room."

"Honest," I said, being serious. "Nobody liked the game."

"Honest," Nik said. "They didn't say anything because they were afraid."

"Honest," Mom said. "You are entitled to your feelings. You are allowed to be pissed off: pissed-off-ness and goodness are not mutually exclusive. In fact, anger can be righteous. Anger can *tell* you something, if you can control it."

"I thought you were worried about me being too intense," I said quietly.

"Anna Maria Hunt. I love every inch of you, and there are *times* to be intense. This is one of them. A kind, honest intensity. Do you hear me?"

I nodded. Mom's anger, Nik's anger, my anger: it was powerful, there, in that room. But I was learning something else, too. My anger didn't have to look like anyone else's. My anger was not tough-as-nails Mom's, or Rachel Riley with a lighter. My anger was *mine*. I would handle it my way.

We made a plan. It feels good, having a plan. I've always been a girl who likes a plan. I had that plan beating in my heart as I crawled into bed that night.

There was a knock on my door just as I was pulling my blankets up to my chin.

"Can I come in?" It was Dad. He gingerly stepped into my room, came over, and sat on the foot of my bed. I sat up a little.

"Mom told me," he said. "Oh, Anna. I'm sorry."

"It's not your fault," I said.

"You can feel like . . . A person can feel helpless, you know?" he said. I did know. It was almost exactly what I'd said to Nik, on this very same bed. "I'm angry. Mom said you're going to try and handle it on your own, and if he does it again, you're going to bring in Mom and tell someone you trust together. I think that sounds like a great plan."

My dad has taught me how to mince a mushroom and how to do algebra, but here is the most important thing he taught me: that there are good, good people in the world. We can't forget that.

"I should have told you guys about the Rachel Riley project," I said. "I didn't know it was going to lead to all of this."

"I think it's leading exactly where it's meant to," he said. "I think you're being very brave."

"Brave enough to let me do the podcasting summit if I get in?"

"Brave enough to *talk* about it, if you get in. Don't worry about that right now."

I yawned. "I don't feel brave. I feel tired."

"You haven't been sleeping, have you? You seem tired all day long."

I shook my head. "It's so quiet and dark here. And besides, my own room . . . I wanted it for a long time, but I got so used to Nik's symphony of snoring. Her computers beeping—they kind of helped me sleep. Plus, you guys go to bed early here."

"Mom's been so busy with her students," Dad said. "She's exhausted at night. Falls right asleep. But I've been working on my laptop pretty late. I've heard you getting up and going to Nik's room."

"You have?" I asked, surprised. "I thought I was the only person awake in the whole house. That was part of why I couldn't fall asleep."

He shook his head. "No, I've just been working from bed. What if I worked in the kitchen? Kept the light on? Then you'd know I was there."

"Do I sound like a baby if I ask you to do that?"

Dad smoothed back my hair and kissed my forehead. "You *are* my baby," he said. And it didn't feel corny or cheesy or anything but right.

Dad went out to work from the kitchen table, and I lay in bed and went over the plan. Exactly what I would say when I saw Trevor Frey tomorrow: *Do not touch me again. If you do, I'm going to report it. It's not funny, and it makes me extremely uncomfortable. Stop.* Don't say *please*, don't ask questions, don't apologize—*demand your dignity*, Mom had said. He only has that freedom because people give it to him.

We do what we've been doing, or we decide to do something different, Nik had said.

I thought of Rachel Riley in that barn, demanding her own dignity, letting that fire burn and burn. Her own anger, and yet, someone else's, too.

Someone else's. Someone else who was targeted by the boys. Someone else who was afraid. Someone else who couldn't use their words to say *stop*, and had to use their actions instead.

Wait.

It couldn't be.

Could it be?

It was. If there was one thing I knew lying there in my bed, it was that truth.

Oh man. Wow. "Wow" is the only word for it. No—"strength," too. *Moxie.* Big, powerful words.

Big, powerful words plus big, powerful actions equals answers. Someone who takes, and someone who takes *back*.

That night, Dad was up until past midnight typing away, and between him and the truth and my own stubborn hope I slept like a rock.

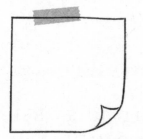

DECEMBER 7

Rachel,

I know about JR.
Meet me at Olin Park after school.
I just want to help.

From, Anna

DECEMBER 7

Anna: This is WHAT HAPPENED TO RACHEL RILEY?: AN INVESTIGATIVE PODCAST by Anna Hunt.

Rachel: Hi.

Anna: Hi.

Rachel: This sucks. This whole year, everything . . . it sucks.

Anna: I know. I'm sorry. You don't have to tell me about it if you don't want to.

Rachel: I thought you were some big podcaster, determined to get to the bottom of things.

Anna: Yeah, well. Mimi Miller cares about people, too. Doesn't just stick a microphone in their face. Maybe I'm switching strategies.

Rachel: How'd you figure it out?

Anna: I knew you were covering for someone. The bike tracks at the barn. And you aren't going to be at our high school next year. That meant you could take

292

the fall for Jordan, pretend you set the fire, and you'd only have to deal with one year of people treating you like complete and utter garbage.

Rachel: But how'd you figure out it was Jordan?

Anna: Everyone kept saying that the boys were so harsh to her. And then I saw the website—

Rachel: The website? How?

Anna: You'd have to ask my sister. She's a tech genius. She helped me bring up the last version of the site before it was wiped. It said that Jordan was going to be . . . the prize. And suddenly, it made sense. The only thing I can't figure out is how she got in.

Rachel: To the barn?

Anna: At first I thought someone just hoisted her in a window, but . . . those windows are high. It's not like she could have brought a ladder on her bike. She had to go in through the door. Right?

Rachel: We had a key.

Anna: A key?

Rachel: Jordan used some passes from Ms. O'Dell's desk to sneak out of the career day assembly when Lana was speaking and stole the key from her coat.

Anna: Wait, but how'd she know—

Rachel: What you have to understand is that the fire really was an accident. She just wanted to switch around the awards cards. She was supposed to win the Rose Award. The plan was that they were going to give her a kiss backstage, right before she went on. There was a whole plan to distract the backstage chaperone—say someone was throwing up in the bathroom or something.

Anna: Wow. They really . . . thought this through.

Rachel: Tell me about it. Maybe if Blake thought that hard in history class he wouldn't have to look over my shoulder every quiz.

Anna: So she thought if someone else won the award . . . problem solved. She wouldn't have to be backstage.

Rachel: Exactly.

Anna: So you went with her?

Rachel: No. I didn't. Not at first. She told me what she was going to do. I was the only person she told. But then, that night . . . she was going to do it in the middle of the night. Sneak out. And I was awake, in my bed, just thinking . . . that it was wrong. That this wasn't the way to handle it. Small lies, hiding from what was going to happen—no. We had to do something, and not this. Because, really, what was that going to solve? We go to school with these creeps. We're going to have to deal with them eventually. They want to get her alone, they'll find a way to get her alone, you know? We had to fix it, not . . . hide. So I got on my bike and rode to

Kincaid at three a.m. I was so scared. I thought every car that passed was going to pull over and abduct me.

Anna: My parents would have killed me.

Rachel: Right. Mine did, afterward. Ha. You're talking to my ghost. But anyway, when I got there, she was just letting herself in.

Anna: What did you say?

Rachel: I followed her. She hadn't seen me yet. She was looking around, probably trying to find a light. She couldn't get the lights on—didn't know where the switches were. That little flashlight on her phone . . . it wasn't enough. It was dark out there, man—you couldn't see anything. There're no streetlights for miles. That kind of dark is so spooky. But there were . . . lanterns. This big decorative lantern in the middle of the room.

Anna: She lit it.

Rachel: For light. Honestly. Just so she could freaking see! There was a lighter there . . . oh my God. She just grabbed it, and lit that lantern, and then she saw me. Oh my gosh, she screamed so loud we started laughing. I started trying to talk to her. Trying to tell her—that I was going to tell on the boys to my mom.

Anna: She'd do something.

Rachel: Yeah. And you know what? It would be fine. It would all be okay. But Jordan . . . She didn't *want anyone to get in trouble. She felt bad.*

Anna: She felt bad? For the boys? That doesn't make any sense.

Rachel: Jordan just never likes to . . . make things messy. She was my best friend. She hated the thought of people thinking she was a person with opinions, or a person with a voice. She just wanted to be nice. Easygoing, *right?*

Anna: My sister said "nice" can be another word for "scared."

Rachel: Last year, she gave Riz Kapoor her homework to copy for an entire semester. She thought he had a hard time doing math. She thought she was being nice. *But he was just lazy! He got a B+ because of her. And still doesn't know how to do long division, probably. She gives things that people don't deserve.*

Anna: Well, people take *things they don't deserve.*

Rachel: They do. Every day. And they will take and take—but they can't take your voice.

Anna: You sound like you're blaming her.

Rachel: No. Not for what happened. Not for the harassment. I always thought that sounded like too big of a word, but . . .

Anna: Me too. I said the same thing.

Rachel: But it is, right? It is *harassment. Anyway, I*

don't blame her for that. At all. But you can't just wish the world into a better place. You have to make it one. You can't control what other people do. But you can control what you do, you know?

Anna: I feel like everyone's been saying that to me lately.

Rachel: It's the truth.

Anna: So, you were talking to her in the barn.

Rachel: Right, and she was freaking out that I was going to tell. She didn't want anyone to know. It's embarrassing, and the boys would all hate her . . . and she started saying stuff that wasn't so nice.

Anna: Like what?

Rachel: She was upset.

Anna: What did she say, Rachel?

Rachel: That—that I was just jealous, that everyone thought I was so uptight. That I probably wanted the Rose Award myself. That I wanted everyone to not like her anymore the way they didn't like me. I got so mad . . . I told her—I told her—

Anna: It's okay.

Rachel: It's not okay. None of this is okay. I told her she was a pushover, and that she cared more about awards than the right thing to do, and that maybe I should just switch the award, because she didn't deserve it.

Anna: Wow.

Rachel: It was the worst fight I've ever gotten in with a friend. And then, I honestly don't know. She was walking, and just kind of tripped, and she hit the lantern and it fell over. The fire happened so fast. There was some kind of cleaning solution on the floor, since they were getting ready for the awards the next day. The place just completely lit up. We didn't have any water or anything. We panicked, and we ran. Ran out the door. Jordan wanted to just keep running, but— this was really, really, really bad. We didn't know what to do. We were watching it burn, completely freaking out, and then . . . sirens. Someone had seen the fire and called 911.

Anna: This sounds scary.

Rachel: I've never been so terrified in my life. We heard someone yelling—like, Hey, are you okay?

Anna: The cops?

Rachel: A neighbor. He was yelling at us to stay put, that it was okay. And Jordan's standing there— still holding the lighter. *She'd never put it down, even when we ran. I looked at her, and her face . . . I can't explain what it was like. Just like every single thing was falling apart. She couldn't believe what she'd done—any of it. And it's all so important to Jordan.*

The way people see her, as so nice and put together, and . . . I couldn't let her do it. Even though she'd said such horrible things about me. I grabbed the lighter from her hand. I told her to run.

Anna: What did she say?

Rachel: No. That I had to come with her. But . . . I had to stay. Someone had to take responsibility. The neighbor'd already seen us. I knew what would happen . . . everyone would hate me. But I could handle it. Jordan couldn't. I told her—Go. Go now. They're coming. I'd do this, if she'd *tell on the boys.* She just jumped on her bike and took off. I stayed. I told the police I was sneaking in to switch the awards card so that I would win the Rose Award, and that I accidentally knocked over a lantern. It was ruled an accidental fire.

Anna: And you wrote the note.

Rachel: I didn't write that note to Blake. I swear.

Anna: But everyone thought you did.

Rachel: Yeah, and Jordan told people that I must have wanted the Rose Award so badly that I'd snuck into the barn, so everyone thought I was a terrible person. A drama queen and a cheater.

Anna: She told everyone that? Even after you covered for her?

Rachel: I texted her the day after the fire and told her that I never wanted to speak to her again. I was . . .

I was really, really hurt. And mad. But if everyone hated her for the fire, she'd never tell anyone about the game. I guess I thought . . . there was still a chance she'd do the right thing.

Anna: But she never did.

Rachel: No. She didn't. I told Cody to make the boys stop, and he deleted the website. I think the fire thing really freaked him out. It made him see how big this whole thing had gotten. And that pretty much put an end to it. There was no awards ceremony, so there was no prize. And now Cody and I are barely even friends. We meet up at Lee's Dairy Emporium sometimes because nobody from our school goes there. I've known him since I was a baby. But . . . it's still happening, and I just feel like he isn't helping it stop. That made me so mad. We got in a fight. So now, yeah—no friends.

<pause>

Anna: You're a good friend.

Rachel: I'm not. Because I still didn't stop it. It's an entire year later, and the game is back.

Anna: Did you ever end up telling your mom? I mean, since you didn't care about your reputation anyway.

Rachel: No. I tried to. But every time I opened my mouth . . .

Anna: You couldn't.

Rachel: I'm a hypocrite. Sitting here, complaining about Jordan. It's not like it's easy to tell people these things. Jordan was my best friend, my entire life. She was the person I was closest to on this entire planet.

Anna: You're a human. She's a human. It's not a car's fault it gets broken into.

Rachel: What?

Anna: Long story.

Rachel: When I heard that the game was back . . . I lost it. I knew I had to do something. And it's not like my social status could fall any further. So I went to the dance.

Anna: That was pretty epic.

Rachel: I should have had someone film it, ha. Maybe if it had gone viral, someone would have given a crap. But what changed? Nothing. My parents even asked Principal Howe about it, and she said she'd reminded teachers about the sexual harassment policy. That's it. That's all!

Anna: It doesn't have to be.

Rachel: What do you mean?

Anna: What if I told you I had an idea?

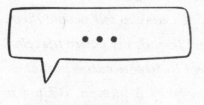

DECEMBER 7

Anna:
Hey. I know this is gonna be a big
surprise. But I know what happened
at the barn. The TRUTH. If you want
to make things right, meet me after
school tomorrow at Lee's Dairy
Emporium. Alone.

Jordan:
I don't know what you think you know

Anna:
I know Rachel's a good friend,
and you owe her this.

DECEMBER 7

To: Katarzyna Kowalski <babciakat@gmail.com>
From: Anna Hunt <ahunt@east.middle.edu>
Subj: YAY!

Babcia,

Mom told me the good news. I can't believe you're coming!
I'm going to give you the grand tour of Madison—ice cream at
Ella's Deli, the Olin Park Christmas lights, every single thing.
When you're here, can we make kołaczki?! Please please
please?!

My Rachel Riley project is . . . going. You're right. I haven't
mentioned it in a while. That's because what started as one
thing kind of turned into another. That happens all the time,

right? People do things with good intentions and a goal in mind. But then it transforms in front of their very eyes.

Rachel Riley is what my English teacher would call an antihero—a person who does the right thing but lacks conventional heroic qualities. She's not loud or even that nice all the time. But she's maybe one of the bravest people I've ever met.

Here's one more fact about penguins, Babcia: they are loyal. Even though they have to travel so many miles sometimes to find food, they return to their homes, over and over and over again.

Love,
Anna

THERE WAS A KNOCK AT THE FRONT DOOR JUST AS we were about to sit down and have dinner. Mom had been telling one of her favorite stories about Babcia growing up. We were all antsy—Babcia was coming, the very next night, on a direct flight from Warsaw to Chicago. Dad would pick her up.

The knock was loud, urgent—the kind of knock where you know you have to answer it; it isn't just someone selling Jesus or vacuums. It wasn't the FedEx guy, who you could kind of half wave at through the window while he strode back to his van. It was a knock-knock-knock of *urgency*, so Nik hopped up to answer it.

Mrs. Boyd stood there, talking fast. Mom hurried to the door. I didn't catch much, but something was wrong—wrong with her, wrong with the baby. Mr. Boyd was out of town for work.

If there's one person you want in your corner during a crisis, it's Mom. She nodded calmly and said a few things to my dad. Mrs. Boyd was crying now, waving her hands, and Mom was grabbing her purse, and Dad was giving me the DoorDash password and sending Nik and me next door to watch Mrs. Boyd's son while they drove her to the emergency room.

Cooper is four. Here are the things I know about four-year-olds:

Literally nothing.

"Um," said Nik, "we're supposed to order pizza . . . Your mom said you hadn't eaten."

"I hate pizza," Cooper said. He was crying, too— he didn't like his mom leaving for the hospital and abandoning him with two strangers. Who would?

"Well, what do you want to eat?" I asked.

"Ice cream," he said.

And maybe it was the wrong thing to do. Maybe we should have called Glass Nickel and ordered a pepperoni pie anyway. But really, is pizza that much healthier than ice cream? So instead, we opened the freezer, found a giant carton of vanilla bean, and spooned some into bowls. The three of us sat at the kitchen table. Cheered up by sugar, Cooper started talking. He told us about preschool, and a mean kid named Michael, who took the truck he wanted, but actually Michael was his best friend in the world, and he loved when they got to go outside, but he didn't like art class, and actually he *did* like art class, as long as he got to draw *Star Wars* characters.

So, add to the list of things I know about four-year-olds: they know how to talk.

"And then," Cooper said, scraping the bottom of his bowl with his spoon, "we got to climb into a fire truck. I didn't want to, because it was big and loud. But I *did* want to because I want to be a fireman."

"So you were brave," Nik said patiently.

"I was scared, and I was brave," said Cooper.

He was completely covered in sugary ice cream soup, so after our spoons *clink-clink*ed against empty bowls, we sent him to wash his hands. He came back with them all sudsy with soap, so I walked him back to rinse them while Nik figured out the TV.

We curled up on the couch in the living room, and Nik pulled up some kind of nature documentary, even though Cooper was begging for *Cars*.

"These are good for you," she told him. "Educational."

"I love the part with the penguins," I said. I'd seen this thing a million times, ever since Dr. Abioye had shown it to me in September. Something about the animals and the soothing British dude's voice helped me do my homework. My penguin research was my favorite part of the year. If my stint as a private eye didn't work out, maybe I'd become a vet. Or a zookeeper.

Nik spread out a fluffy red afghan over me, her, and Cooper. I sat in the middle. For all his requests for Lightning McQueen, he instantly loved it—the shots of giant polar bears, catching fish with their enormous paws.

"This is where it starts," Nik said after a few minutes, nodding toward one of the emperor penguins. "The penguin part. Did you know they've found skeletons of penguins that were six feet tall? That's a Dad-sized penguin."

"I've been reading about penguins all year. I'm basically a penguin savant."

Her phone buzzed, and she glanced at it.

"Bronson?" I asked.

"No," she said. "Heather. One of my friends from CodeHERs. You met her . . . pink hair? Bronson doesn't text me anymore."

"He stopped?" I asked.

"I told him to stop calling me," she said. "I told him to leave me alone. And I said it like I meant it."

Nik: hacker of websites, defeater of demons.

"This is where it starts," she said again.

18

RILEY FAMILY HOLIDAY LETTER
DECEMBER 8

❄ ❄ ❄

HO-HO-HO and MERRY CHRISTMAS!

This year has been a busy one for the Riley family. Kristy and Todd's graphic design business continues to flourish, and we've taken on more clients than ever before. Rachel has excelled academically as well as musically—she's made it to the final round of applicants for the Moorland Academy of the Arts, and we're crossing our fingers that this lifetime dream becomes a reality for her. Although this year hasn't been without its challenges, we're as thankful as ever for the friends who've stood by us and the hope and peace that come from this time of year.

With love,
Kristy, Todd, and Rachel Riley

JORDAN GOT TO LEE'S FIRST. I SAW HER THERE, WAIT-ing for me, and she looked terrified. But she still looked put together, like always, in a pink puffer jacket and her hair in a French braid.

I stepped inside and felt the warm blast of the heater smack me in my face. Lee's was practically empty—not a lot of people wanted ice cream in twenty-degree weather. The little bells sang, announcing someone was entering, and Jordan jumped about a foot in the air. The two cashiers behind the register were comparing manicures.

"Hi," I said, going to sit at her table. She had a milkshake in front of her.

"Hi," she said quietly.

"What did you get?"

"A mint chip shake. Want some? It's good." Jordan offering me her shake kind of reminded me of Blake at Harvest Fest—the way he just took popcorn, with-out asking.

"I'm okay," I told her. "You should have let me treat. I have a gift card."

"Don't be nice to me," she muttered. "I don't deserve it, and you know it. How did you figure it out? Did Rachel tell you?"

"No," I said. "I just . . . figured it out. Took a chance. And it turns out I was right."

She picked at her thumbnail, not meeting my eyes. "Look . . . I know what I did was horrible. Last year was really, really hard on me."

"I know."

She glanced up. "Are you going to put all of this in your podcast camp application or whatever?"

"Um . . . I'm not sure yet." The truth was, the podcasting summit was the last thing on my mind. This *thing*, this question of what happened to Rachel Riley, had taken on such a new form. I guess that's what happens when you open a can of worms—a mess pours out and takes you in a thousand directions. You wish there were easy answers, quick and simple solutions. But most of the time, there's one person's needs and another person's wants and a collision of it all.

"You can," she said, looking out the window. "I think . . . I sort of think it's time people knew the truth. Rachel doesn't deserve this."

"*Nobody* does," I said. "A lot of things have been happening that nobody deserves."

She nodded. "If I could do things different . . . I would."

"Like what?"

"I don't know," she said. "Say something sooner. The whole switching-the-awards thing . . . I kind of knew that wasn't going to work. It was a dumb plan. And then when the fire happened, I shouldn't have let Rachel take the fall. Even though she *told* me to. I should have admitted it was my fault. This year, everyone was so mean to her, and it was all my fault. I said mean things to her, and about her, and I'm not a mean person. Not usually. Not ever!"

"She said you didn't exactly hold up your end of the bargain, either. With the game. You didn't tell anyone."

Jordan looked down at her shake and wiggled her straw a bit. "When everyone around you seems to think something's fine, it's hard to say that you *don't* think it's fine."

"Rachel didn't think it was fine, either," I said. "Neither did Kaylee. They both told me."

Jordan bit her lip. "We should have talked about it more."

"Probably. But it also wasn't your fault."

"No. That's true." She took her straw and mixed around the melting remains of her shake a little. "I could have said something, though. And now it feels like it's too late."

"It's not." We both looked up—another voice. There she was—Rachel Riley, pulling off her earmuffs.

19

DECEMBER 12

MOORLAND ACADEMY OF THE ARTS

Intellectual Growth Through Creative Expression

Rachel Riley,

Congratulations! You are being offered admission to Moorland Academy of the Arts for your high school education, beginning this autumn.

Term will begin September 1. Attached, you will find instructions for registration and class selection, as well as a detailed packet on tuition and financial assistance.

We look forward to seeing you in September.

Sincerely,
Catherine Fiorelli
Headmistress

DECEMBER 13

To: LIST: Parents of East Eighth Graders

From: Inaya Fayen <ifayen@east.middle.edu>

Subj: Updates to East Middle School Harassment Policy

Parents,

My name is Inaya Fayen, and I'm the guidance counselor at
East Middle. I've had the good fortune of meeting some of you
in person, but unfortunately, not all of you. I'm writing to you
today to make you aware of some incidents that have recently
been revealed to the administration of East Middle and some
steps we're taking to rectify the situation.

It's been made clear to myself and Lila Howe that instances of
sexual harassment have been occurring within our hallways
steadily over the past year. This includes a game wherein the

male students have inappropriate physical conduct with the female students. Regretfully, we must admit that although East Middle has a very strict sexual harassment policy on paper, we did not take the proper steps to put an end to the harassment. For that, you have the fullest apology from our administration and staff.

Yesterday, we held a community meeting with our eighth-grade class, with myself as facilitator. The victims were given a chance to speak voluntarily, and the boys accused of harassment were invited to respond. We had an open, productive listening session, followed by a dialogue.

I enlisted the help of a couple of our students to rewrite our sexual harassment policy, which I have attached here. Please review it with your student and return it, signed by the student, by the end of the week. If you have any questions, concerns, or comments, my door is always open.

Best,
Inaya Fayen, PhD
Guidance Counselor
East Middle School

DECEMBER 13

Kaylee:
How did you think the meeting went
yesterday??

Jordan:
It was good. I liked being
able to say how I felt
being the "prize." I think
the guys were kinda
surprised.

Kaylee:
I was surprised too.

Jordan:
You were???

Kaylee:
Idk. You always made it seem like you
didn't take it that seriously. I didn't know
how upset it made you. It made me
really upset too. We could have talked
about it more. I'm sad we didn't.

Jordan:
We can now 🖤 Besties
for the resties, right?

Kaylee:
DUH. 😍

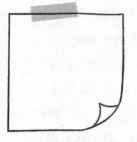

DECEMBER 13

To the girls of East Middle School,

We are very sorry for our behavior over the past
year. We know now that something we thought was
funny wasn't funny at all to you. You said in the
meeting that we made you feel small, scared, and
unsafe. We appreciate you giving the chance for us
to ask forgiveness and make amends.

These are the changes we will be making going
forward:

We will all sign the new sexual harassment policy
we, as a class, crafted together in the community
meeting, which we believe is fair.

We will voluntarily serve four weeks of after-
school detention, where we will read and discuss
material on sexual harassment provided by Ms. O'Dell.

We will commit to making East Middle School a safe place for all by stopping the harassment immediately and holding each other accountable.

For the February bake sale, we will not use the money for new baseball uniforms as we had planned and instead donate the funds to the National Alliance to End Sexual Violence.

If you have any other requests from us, we would be happy to discuss them.

We would also like to thank Dr. Abioye and Dr. Fayen for helping us write this letter.

Sincerely,
Blake Wyatt
Trevor Frey
Carlos Agnelli
Cody McLeen
Riz Kapoor

Official Sexual Harassment Policy from the East Middle School Handbook

East Middle School prohibits any form of sexual harassment by all persons within the school district, including, but not limited to, students and staff. This policy applies to conduct during and related to the operation of East Middle School.

Harassment will not be tolerated under any circumstance. "Sexual harassment" is defined here as repetitive unwelcome behavior of a sexual nature that creates an intimidating or hostile educational environment or interferes with an individual's work or academic performance. Sexual harassment examples include, but are not limited to:

- Sexual slurs, threats, inappropriate remarks, derogatory comments
- Graphic verbal comments about an individual's body
- Sexual jokes, drawings, or pictures
- Spreading of sexual rumors
- Unwelcome touching of an individual's body or clothing in a sexual manner

East Middle School will take all necessary steps to put an end to sexual harassment of anyone in school and at school-sponsored activities. If harassment is reported, it will be investigated to the fullest extent of our school bylaws. East Middle expects all harassment to be promptly reported to a staff member. Within twenty-four hours, that staff member must notify both the principal and guidance counselor. Any staff member who does not notify the principal and guidance counselor within twenty-four hours of witnessing sexual harassment or receiving a sexual harassment report will face punishment. During the investigation, both the alleged harasser and victim will be given an opportunity to present witnesses and/or evidence. If harassment is found to have taken place, the harassing student will be immediately suspended for a minimum of three days and be required to submit a formal apology.

East Middle School prohibits any retaliatory behavior against any complainant. Initiations of sexual harassment claims will not reflect negatively on the complainant, and any harasser who is found to be retaliating against a complainant will face further punishment in the form of suspension or expulsion.

DECEMBER 14

To: Rachel Riley <rriley@east.middle.edu>
CC: Kristy Riley <kristy.riley@rileygraphics.com>
From: Principal Lila Howe <lhowe@east.middle.edu>
Subj: Apology

Rachel,

Our motto here at East Middle School is "Peace begins with us."

As the principal of our school, I should be the living emblem of that motto. If peace begins with anyone, it should begin with me, the leader of our school.

Instead, I failed to listen to your experiences and your proof. When I heard at our community meeting that you didn't trust the staff at East Middle to protect the students, I knew where that failure lay: on myself.

I am sorry that I contributed to your negative experiences at East Middle. I do hope that next year at Moorland, you are able to make as positive a change as you made here at our school. Your resilience has inspired me, even though I'm truly sad it was needed.

All my best,
Principal Howe

"WHAT'S A COMMUNITY MEETING?" NIK ASKED.

We were at Glass Nickel, eating a massive pizza, and I was happy. Why? Babcia. Babcia, Babcia, Babcia—sitting right there, across from me, eating her slice of pepperoni with a knife and fork. Your people make you feel like *you*. And these were my people.

"So, the guidance counselor led it after Rachel, Jordan, and I talked to her. But we got to ask any other teachers we wanted. We picked Ms. O'Dell and Dr. Abioye, the science teacher," I explained. "And then the girls all got a chance to talk. Whoever wanted to. And once it started . . . it just went, and went. I was kind of afraid nobody would say anything. But it's like . . . seeing the other girls talk made some of the quieter girls brave. And suddenly *everyone* was sharing their stories. It wasn't as cheesy as it sounds."

"It doesn't sound cheesy," Dad said. "It sounds powerful." He waved over the waitress and asked for more napkins.

"Yeah, well. We'll see what happens." I shrugged.

"The boys just had to listen. They couldn't say anything! And some of them looked kind of annoyed, but some of them really paid attention. I could tell."

"Did they get to respond?" Mom asked. Always the lawyer.

"Yeah," I said. "After they listened to every single girl, they could respond. It was . . . interesting. Mostly, they just said they thought they were kidding and they didn't know, but that they understood now. Then we all worked together on a new sexual harassment policy, and the boys worked with Dr. Abioye to write us a letter of apology. I mean, who knows? Maybe nothing will change."

"Maybe it will," said Babcia in her thick Polish accent, pointing her fork at me.

"It's hard to say," I admitted. "When things have been the same and the same and the same . . ."

She shook her head. "Don't you think people felt that way throughout all of history, Anna Maria? Communism!"

Mom glanced at her watch. "Congratulations, we made it twenty-three minutes without a mention of communism. World record for you, Mom." Babcia bumped her shoulder. Mothers, daughters—doesn't matter how old you are. Like I said, they *know* you.

"Katarzyna's right," Dad said. "You think people

watching tanks roll down their streets thought things could change? Or, hello—Jim Crow laws?"

"The people in Japanese internment camps?" asked Nik.

"Women getting the right to *vote*?" Mom chimed in.

"You don't *wish* for the change," Babcia said. "You *make* the change, and then you hope. Hope in something bigger than yourself."

Suddenly, someone tapped on my shoulder. I turned to see Cody McLeen, son of the Wedding Queen, standing there.

"Hey," I said, surprised.

"Hi," he said. "I'm here with my family."

"Same." I gestured at the table.

"I was wondering . . . if we could talk for a second," he said.

I glanced at my parents, who nodded, curious. Then I followed Cody outside, into the frigid December air.

"Sorry," he said, blowing into his hands. "It's cold out here. I won't—I didn't mean to bug you. I just had to tell you something."

I nodded.

"Jordan didn't take the key," he mumbled.

"What?"

"The key," he said a little more loudly. "To the

barn. Rachel told me that's what you thought happened. She couldn't find it—she thought it'd be in my mom's coat, where she keeps her car keys. But she has a different key ring in her purse for venues. I saw Jordan trying to find it when I was going to the bathroom. Then as my mom was leaving, I walked her to her car, and snuck the key ring out of her purse. The Kincaid events barn key had a cow on it. It wasn't exactly a secret. I took it off her key ring and gave it to Jordan."

I stared at him, and it all came together. A complicated puzzle that I'd found the middle pieces to.

Click. Who had been slipping clues into my locker, trying to help me?

Click. Who had written Blake that note, demanding he stop the game?

Click. Who had known all along that it was Jordan who had actually started the barn fire?

"You," I said.

"Me," he said.

"You should have said something sooner."

"I know." He looked down the street. Snow was starting to fall, just barely. "I'm saying something now."

"Does Rachel know?" I asked.

"I'm not sure," he said. "I guess I was just . . .

scared. I wanted to make it up to Rachel. I wanted to help you find out the truth."

"It doesn't work like that," I said. A huge truck drove past us, splattering some gray snow and slush onto the sidewalk as we stepped out of the way. "Actions don't just cancel each other out. You just . . . You do what you do, until you decide to do something differently."

"So what can I do differently?" he asked.

"You do what you guys wrote in that letter, and you *help*," I said. "Principal Howe telling people to cut it out is one thing. The boys telling each other to cut it out is another."

Cody nodded. "Okay. I can do that."

"Okay."

"You think I'm a jerk, don't you?" he asked. Not angrily or anything. Just like it was a fact.

I shrugged. "Does it matter?"

"No," he said. "I guess it doesn't."

"I should get back inside."

"Me too. Bye, Anna."

"Bye, Cody."

20

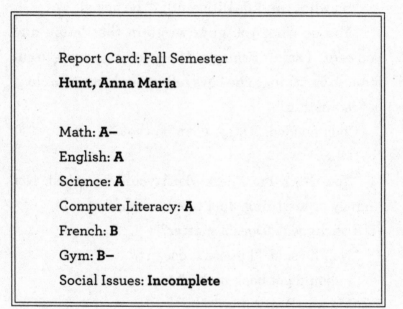

Report Card: Fall Semester
Hunt, Anna Maria

Math: **A–**
English: **A**
Science: **A**
Computer Literacy: **A**
French: **B**
Gym: **B–**
Social Issues: **Incomplete**

DECEMBER 17

Cody:
I heard about Moorland. Your mom told
my mom. Congratulations.

Cody:
I won't forget the magic trees.

:
Me neither.

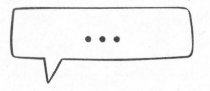

DECEMBER 19

Cody:
Hey Anna. I thought these texts might help with your project.

Anna:
Oh, wow. Thanks!

Cody:
I should be the one saying thanks to you I think. Haha

DECEMBER 20

Kaylee:
Hey, I just slipped something in your
locker. It's a notebook that me + Jordan
use to write notes in . . . we thought
some of the stuff might kinda help with
your podcast. Sorry. We weren't sure if
we wanted to share it but we think it's
important.

DECEMBER 20

Rachel:
Cody asked if he could send you our
texts to help with your podcast thing. I
said yes. I also wanted to give you some
of the stuff I sent Moorland, so I put that
in your locker, too. And the lighter in the
bag . . . you can have it. I can't believe
they never took it from me. Also, just
so you know, I'm not coming back to
school after break. I'm gonna do virtual
school so I can focus more on violin and
get ready for my new school. I will never
forget you, Anna Hunt, even though
you're incredibly weird. 🙂

DECEMBER 21

To: Anna Hunt <ahunt@east.middle.edu>

From: Northwestern University Campus For Kids

<campusforkids@northwestern.edu>

Subj: Your Application Has Been Received

ANNA HUNT,

Thank you for your application to our teen podcasting summit. Accepted podcasters will be notified by March of this year.

In the meantime, make sure to follow Mimi Miller on social media—@mimimiller on all platforms!

Next year, Mimi will be launching Curious Cast, a new podcasting network for teen-run shows. As an applicant to our program, you'll have first access to these new shows, and may even be invited to create one. Mimi and the Campus for Kids program at Northwestern believe that kids can change the world, if they're brave enough to try, and that the truth is always something worth chasing.

Thank you for applying to join us this summer.

DECEMBER 21

To: Anna Hunt <ahunt@east.middle.edu>

From: Alicia O'Dell <aodell@east.middle.edu>

Subj: Your Incomplete grade

Anna,

I'm aware that you did, in fact, turn in your un-essay. But a few pieces of metal glued to a piece of paper does not an un-essay make, and your presentation, where you proceeded to just read "The Road Less Traveled," was sorely lacking. (That poem isn't even about conservation, Anna, and trying to connect the beauty of Frost's words to a message about driving less to save energy was quite a stretch.)

I hold my students to a high standard because I know they're capable of meeting it. After having you in class for a semester,

I believe you to be a bright, passionate girl who cares about a lot of social issues. Teachers aren't blind. I have a strong feeling you have another project you've been working on on the side. Why don't you show me *that* project, and I'll adjust your grade accordingly. If you choose not to do so, that's perfectly fine, but I'll be forced to give your un-essay on recycling the grade it deserved.

Sincerely,
Ms. O'Dell

JANUARY 9

IT WAS A HIGH SCHOOL BASKETBALL GAME.

Loud and echoey, smelling like sweat. Not my favorite place to be, honestly. I know there are Sports People who would gladly spend every night watching people try to get balls into hoops—not really my choice of entertainment. But Bee invited me, and I didn't have anything else to do. Her mom dropped us off, and my mom was going to pick us up. We were pretty good friends, now, and Nik was right—it felt good to join the world. When I found out she'd never seen any of the *Harry Potter* movies, I'd invited her over for a winter break movie marathon, and on New Year's, she slept over at our house so her parents could go to Milwaukee for a party.

I'd joined Global Leaders, too. I convinced Elizabeth-and-Malika that they needed a vice president of local issues to help our very own school improve, in addition to the wider world. Ms. O'Dell loved the idea. So while we definitely weren't Elizabeth-and-Malika-and-Anna, we always waved at each other in the halls, and sometimes I sat with them at lunch when I wasn't in the mood to read.

But the best news? The email sitting in my inbox, telling me my podcasting summit application had been submitted. Even if I didn't get in, I knew I had made something Mimi Miller–worthy. And that was pretty cool.

"Okay, *this* I can get behind," I said, sucking down a blue slushy. I had pretzel balls, too. Sports? Whatever. Concession stands? All about them.

Bee rolled her eyes. "Do you even know who we're playing?" I didn't. But we were sitting with some other kids from school—Kaylee was there, and she and Jordan and Chelsea were laughing about some dumb thing the art teacher had said last week. Josie Goldberg was there, a girl from my algebra class, who I didn't know that well, but I saw a faded copy of a book I read last year poking out of her canvas bag one day. I asked her if she was done with it, and she told me she'd read it six times. She brought a book everywhere, just in case she got bored. I *loved* that. So I was laughing. Friends—I was doing it. I was.

Bee had invited Rachel, but she was visiting her grandparents that weekend. She was going to be homeschooled the rest of the year so that she could spend her afternoons in one-on-one violin lessons. Rachel Riley had made her mark on East Middle, and now she was gone—sailing away on the wind like Mary Poppins. She hadn't said goodbye. I wish I could say we stayed in touch, but we didn't. In fact, I never saw her again.

I just happened to glance up at that moment, about halfway through the second quarter—who knows why? I was probably wondering if I needed nachos, too. Nacho cheese is one of those foods you're not supposed to like but I love. And that's when I saw it. Trevor Frey, leaning over to Malika's bra strap—he grabbed it, and snapped it.

My heart fell a million stories. Nothing had changed. *Nothing.* That community meeting, our words—they'd been completely pointless. Rachel was right. Words didn't work. Nobody cared. This tale as old as time was going to keep on going, with a straight line from Poe to Picasso to Trevor. I thought of Babcia at Glass Nickel, convincing me that even the most hopeless things weren't so hopeless after all. Rachel Riley's sacrifice and Jordan Russell's bravery had both been for nothing.

Well, Babcia was wrong. There was still communism and human trafficking and butts being slapped and bras being snapped. I wanted to walk right over to Malika and quit Global Leaders, right then and there. Dedicating time to something that could never change—why would a person do that?

But then . . . something else. Riz Kapoor. His hair was flopping in his eyes. He had been sitting two rows back, with Blake. He bounded down the bleachers, stepping over Lia and Carmen. The echoey noise of his feet against wood seemed extra loud—louder than the squeaks of basketball shoes, louder than the referee's whistle calling a foul. Riz leaned over, said something to Trevor. He was smiling, but his eyes were serious. Malika said something, too. She wasn't smiling. But she was *there*.

Trevor turned to Malika. Mumbled something. Riz fist-bumped him. Malika nodded.

Took a sip of her pop.

Went back to talking to Elizabeth.

Riz and Trevor started talking about something else. And maybe Malika would report it. Or maybe they'd become friends. Or maybe she'd carry a secret shame around for years and years and years, but the point was that she didn't *have* to. There were options. Options we'd created. Choices in front of her, lined up like bread crumbs, taking her to where she wanted to go.

And it was there, in the sweat and stench of a gym. There in the bleachers, the crappy wooden kind that give you splinters in your butt.

Change. It *was* there, after all.

You could see it, if you squinted. You could feel it, if you sat still.

You could create it, if you tried.

ACKNOWLEDGMENTS

WHEN EVERYONE TALKS ABOUT THEIR "DREAM JOB" AS A kid, I'm so fortunate to say I actually *have* mine. Thank you, Jesus, for this windy path you've gifted me.

Alyssa Miele, editor extraordinaire: third time's the charm. Thanks for creating art with me and putting up with my complicated book timelines.

Alex Slater—in an industry that isn't always transparent or straightforward, you're the best guide a girl could ask for.

Thank you to Janet Rosenberg, Rye White, Kim Craskey, and Sonja West and the many others at Quill Tree who assisted with Anna's story. Thanks also to Helen Crawford-White, the artist who designed the stunning cover!

Thank you to the many friends in my life who've taught me the meaning of loyalty. In particular, thanks to Emily Linn—you are the epitome of a friend, and I'm so grateful to you.

This book wouldn't have been written without the team at Almost Home Childcare Center—so thank you to Miss Di,

Miss McKenna, Miss Casey, Miss Taira, Miss Heidi, Miss Niki, and all of the other caregivers who love my kiddos so well.

The majority of this book was written in Whelan's Coffee & Ice Cream and Roots Coffee Bar. Thanks to all of the baristas who keep the coffee refills coming!

My brothers and sisters will instantly flip to the acknowledgements to make sure they're named. I love all of you goons: Paul, Mary Grace, John, Jenna, Ellie, Cole, and Asia. You make writing sibling stories so ridiculously easy. To my nieces and nephew, Nora, Otis, and Josie Courchane: thanks for the snuggles and joy.

My parents are my safe place to land and endless encouragers. Mark and Grace Courchane, there isn't enough space here to tell you what you mean to me.

Krzysztof Swinarski, defender of truth and fixer of broken snow blowers: where would I be without you? Double thanks on this particular book for helping me turn Nik into a great coder and Anna into an authentic Pole.

To my son, Benjamin: I hope and pray you become the type of leader the world needs.

And to my daughters, Teresa and Bridget: I hope and pray that you stay courageous, rooted, and kind.